Tales of the
Scottish Highlands

Tales of the Scottish Highlands

Collected and retold by
GERALD WARNER

Illustrations by pupils of the
Lochgilphead High School
under the guidance of
John Leckie

SHEPHEARD-WALWYN

ISBN 0 85683 061 5

Printed and bound in Great Britain
for Shepheard-Walwyn (Publishers) Ltd,
26 Charing Cross Road (Suite 34), London WC2H 0DH
by Cox & Wyman Ltd, Reading, Berkshire,
from typesetting by Alacrity Phototypesetters
Banwell Castle, Weston-super-Mare

Cover design by Alan Downs
based on illustration by W.B. Taylor

2nd impression, 1987

Acknowledgements

I should like to thank Mr. John Leckie, Principal Teacher of Art at Lochgilphead High School, and his pupils, for the very attractive and atmospheric drawings which they kindly supplied as illustrations. My thanks are also extended to those pupils at Lochgilphead whose drawings had to be excluded due to lack of space; to Mr. Duncan Ferguson, whose good offices were instrumental in arranging this artistic co-operation; to the late Mrs. Margaret Earl and Mr. John Carmichael, who helpfully supplied folklore material; to the Rev. Professor Murdo Macdonald, for updating the collection by contributing 'A Phantom Motor-Car', and to Catriona Montgomery for help with Gaelic material.

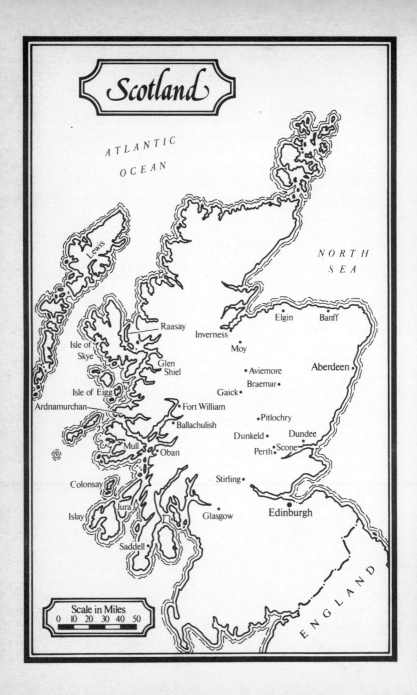

Acknowledgements

I should like to thank Mr. John Leckie, Principal Teacher of Art at Lochgilphead High School, and his pupils, for the very attractive and atmospheric drawings which they kindly supplied as illustrations. My thanks are also extended to those pupils at Lochgilphead whose drawings had to be excluded due to lack of space; to Mr. Duncan Ferguson, whose good offices were instrumental in arranging this artistic co-operation; to the late Mrs. Margaret Earl and Mr. John Carmichael, who helpfully supplied folklore material; to the Rev. Professor Murdo Macdonald, for updating the collection by contributing 'A Phantom Motor-Car', and to Catriona Montgomery for help with Gaelic material.

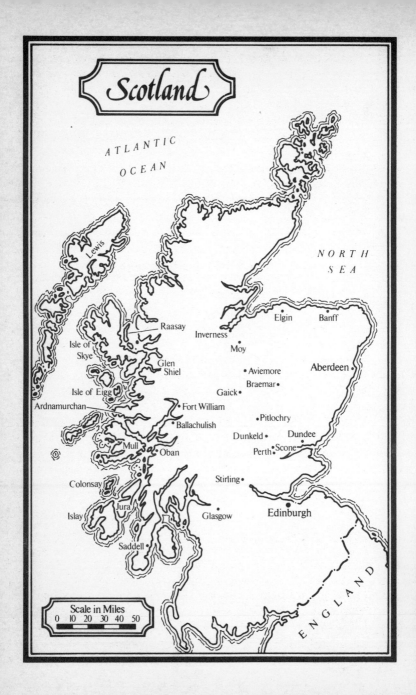

Introduction

The rich traditions of Highland folklore amount to a cultural treasury of almost unlimited resources, but what is perhaps too seldom appreciated is the variety, as well as the volume, of this heritage. In this collection, therefore, priority has been given to presenting a balanced representation of the different strands of Highland culture.

First and foremost, there are the stories of everyday life traditionally told around the peat fire; tales with a background of agrarian scenes and agricultural implements. Then there are the heroic legends of famous warriors and chieftains, but still with many homely touches which betray the modest origins of the original narrators. Since Highland life has always been imbued with a strongly mystical vein, there are also many traditions concerning the Devil, witches, warlocks, ghostly apparitions and malevolent fairies. To base these flights of fancy securely in a world of reality, however, many narratives of factual Highland history have been included, as a reminder that this apparently remote world of islands, mountains, peat-bogs and glens was also the stage on which were enacted many events of crucial significance in Scotland's development as a nation.

It is not only in their subject matter that the stories exhibit wide variety: the broadest possible geographical spread has also been sought, from distant St. Kilda to the southerly reaches of the Mull of Kintyre. The origins of the different narratives are varied too, ranging from enduring oral tradition (for example 'A Royal Peat-Gatherer') to more conventional historical research (such as the reconstruction of events which describes 'Scotland's Last Coronation').

Particular attention has been paid to rehabilitating those stories and traditions which were unearthed by folklorists in the nineteenth century and subsequently neglected. The selection of material has inevitably been to some extent arbitrary, due to the limitations of a single volume. Some people may be disgruntled to find stories omitted which seem to them indispensable in a collection which aspires to be representative of Highland tradition. Such preferences, however, are necessarily subjective and the present selection also attempts to bring to light some previously obscure material, as well as re-telling the familiar legends.

The principal aim, of course, is the fundamental purpose of all story-telling — the engagement and entertainment of the reader.

Gerald Warner
August 1982

GENERAL HIGHLAND TALES

A Missing Husband

Ronald Macdonell, a cadet of the house of Keppoch, was tacksman of Inch, a farm on the banks of the River Spean, almost opposite Keppoch. He was a brave, soldierly fellow, highly esteemed in the district. In the course of time, he fell in love with the daughter of the chief of the MacMartin Camerons of Letterfinlay — Eilidh *na Leitreach* — and she loved him in return. Her father, however, had hopes of securing a richer husband for his lovely daughter, so he made her youthfulness a pretext to put off their betrothal and in the meantime other suitors sought Eilidh's hand in vain.

One evening, Ronald and his men were returning from a day's hunting, when they heard a woman's scream on the hillside. Ronald's followers froze in their tracks, thinking it the cry of the *bean-shith*, but he had recognised Eilidh's voice and ordered them to follow him instantly. Rounding some rocks, he came upon a cadet of the house of Mackintosh, a man whose offer of marriage had recently been turned down by Eilidh, attempting to abduct the girl. Ronald and his party fell upon Mackintosh and his retainers, routing them after a desperate struggle. Mackintosh himself escaped, vowing revenge on Ronald. Eilidh clung gratefully to her lover and they returned together to her father's house.

No sooner had Ronald crossed the threshold of Letterfinlay House, however, than he fell down in a swoon. It was then discovered that he had a ghastly wound across his forehead, so that he was lucky to be alive. For weeks he lay ill at Letterfinlay, lovingly nursed by Eilidh, and at the end of his convalescence her father had no option but to give his consent to their marriage. So Ronald returned to Inch, deliriously happy, with his young bride who, before a year had passed, bore him a daughter to whom they gave the name Mariot.

Not long after, Ronald had to travel south on business. Even this brief separation from his beloved wife was a misery to him, but he promised to return as quickly as possible. His best friend and

11

kinsman, a young man named Coll, was staying at Inch, and Ronald charged him with protecting his wife and child. On the morning of his departure, Coll was standing with the baby in his arms. 'If I do not return,' Ronald asked laughingly, 'which will you marry — my wife or my daughter?'

The young lad, laughing himself, replied, 'Perhaps both!'

Weeks passed, until Ronald's return was long overdue. Eilidh began to grow anxious and, as the weeks grew into months, desperate. Night after night, she sat up into the small hours, listening for the sound of his return. Eventually the months became years, hope perished, and she no longer expected her husband. All this time, Coll stayed on at Inch, faithful to his charge, protecting Eilidh and Mariot.

His protection was needed, for, seeing Ronald given up for dead, Mackintosh began again to pay court to Eilidh. She lived in dire fear of him and at last, partly to escape his attentions and partly to reward the devotion of her late husband's friend, she decided to marry Coll. In any case, Mariot was now nearly sixteen and she needed a father to supervise her own marriage, which must surely come about in the near future. So, a day was set for the wedding of Eilidh and Coll, everyone in the neighbourhood agreeing that it was a very suitable arrangement.

On the day of the wedding, a weary and dust-caked traveller arrived in the district and stopped to request a glass of water at a roadside cottage. The woman of the house, eager to retail local gossip, told him of the great festivities that day at the house of Inch, and what wedding it was. The traveller then made his way to Inch and asked for food; since the hospitality there was particularly lavish that day, he was given a more than generous meal. He asked if the marriage ceremony was over, and was told that it was.

'Will you ask the bride,' he said, 'to do me the honour of giving me a glass of whisky out of her own hand, and I will give her my blessing.'

When Eilidh was told of the stranger's request, she gladly came in, still looking young and beautiful, filled a glass with whisky and handed it to the unknown guest. He stood up and gazed at her, apparently tongue-tied, though he seemed to be making efforts to speak. He took off his bonnet and ran his fingers through his hair, exposing his brow. Then Eilidh saw there the terrible scar left by Mackintosh's sword and she recognised Ronald.

12

'My darling! My darling!' she cried, throwing herself into his arms.

Within minutes, the wedding guests knew that the ceremony they had just witnessed was null and void. Coll accepted the return of Ronald in a spirit of noble generosity. But he was not to be left disconsolate. 'Come here, my friend,' said Ronald to his faithful young kinsman. 'You cannot have my wife, but I have heard today of your loyalty, and you shall have my daughter.'

Now, it happened that Mariot secretly loved Coll and had been in despair over his marriage to her mother. To her joy, this unexpected turn of events reversed her ill fortune and secured her the happiness she longed for. So the priest came in once more and performed a second marriage. When it was over and all the company were drinking the health of the happy couple, Ronald exclaimed to Coll, 'By my garment, you kept your word! You said that, if I did not return, you would marry both my wife and daughter. But it was too bad to marry them both on the same day!'

One question remained uppermost in the minds of all those present: what had kept Ronald away from home for fifteen long years? Gradually it became known that he had been the victim of a great wrong and that his enforced absence had been the result of some treachery perpetrated by Mackintosh. Ronald himself refused to be drawn on the subject, confiding only to those closest to him that he feared, if the full story became known, that the fiery cross would be sent round to call Clan Donald to bloody war against the Mackintoshes. Now that he was safely home, all he desired was a peaceful life. Ronald and Eilidh had several more children after that, and the marriage of Coll and Mariot was also fruitful. Since they were granted the peace they hoped for, the reunited couple lived together in great happiness, watching their children and grandchildren playing together round the same hearth.

Young MacCulloch's Wooing

There was a flourishing family called MacCulloch, much respected in Cromarty for two centuries, but eventually extinct, whose fortunes had been founded on a clever stratagem. The first of the line was a boy named Alastair, who had to leave home in search of work when his mother was widowed. He found employment on the farm of a very rich old tacksman in Cromarty. During his first few weeks with his new household, Alastair cut a poor enough figure, for he had lately grown so apprehensive about his future and lived so much in fear of poverty that his manner had become dour and taciturn. This was not his natural character, however, and once he began to settle down and feel secure, he gradually relaxed and earned the affection of his master and his family by not only performing his duties diligently, but also enlivening the place with his wit and practical jokes.

At this time, Alastair was fourteen years old and his master, a widower, had a pretty daughter of nineteen. Despite his tender years, Alastair soon fell head-over-heels in love with Lillias, which was small wonder, for half the youths in the parish were eager to marry her. She, for her part, had no interest in any of them, and least of all in her father's herd-boy, five years younger than herself. Alastair knew that his chances of wooing his master's daughter were slim indeed, at least for the foreseeable future, but he consoled himself with the thought that he had no successful rival as yet, and he spent much of his time in daydreaming about Lillias. In the evenings, he would sit in a corner, watching the light of the peat-fire flickering on the face of the girl he loved; the gentle courtesy he showed towards her earned him the approval of her family.

But the time was coming when young Alastair would be able to do something more positive than dream about his love. Indeed, his fertile imagination and his skill in playing practical jokes were to stand him in good stead. It was coming up to Hallowe'en of the year 1560, and the young people of the district were planning the games that they would play. Alastair overheard Lillias discussing the night's festivities with another girl, the daughter of a neighbouring farmer.

'Will you really venture on throwing the clue?' he heard their

14

neighbour ask. 'The kiln, ye ken, is dark and lonely, and there's mony a story no' true if folk havenae often been frightened.'

'Throw it? Oh, surely!' replied Lillias. 'Who would think it worthwhile to harm the like o' me? Besides, you can bide for me just a wee bittie aff. I'd like to know the name o' my gudeman, or whether I'm tae get a gudeman at all.'

From this, Alastair guessed that his beloved was going to play an old Hallowe'en game, to find out the name of her future husband, in the old kiln nearby. So he went to his master and asked leave to spend the night of Hallowe'en with some other young folk on a neighbouring farm. This permission he got without difficulty. When the evening of Hallowe'en came, therefore, he said goodbye to the rest of the household, wishing them good sport, and set off very publicly for his friends' cottage.

As soon as he was well out of sight of home, he doubled back furtively to the kiln, scaled its circular gable, heaved himself inside through the chimney and sat down among the cold ashes of the furnace. He then waited uncomfortably for an hour. At last he heard light footsteps, the door was unlocked and Lillias appeared in the pale shaft of moonlight that shone across the threshold. Nervously, she took out a small clue of yarn, which she threw towards the furnace where Alastair was concealed, and at once began to wind it in again. Alastair allowed the yarn to revolve among the ashes until it was half wound-in, then he laid hold of it with his hand. Feeling resistance, which she had scarcely believed would materialise, Lillias stammered the ritual question, 'Wha hauds?'

'Alastair MacCulloch,' was the reply, from the darkness.

Lillias turned and ran from the kiln, leaving the door open. Alastair remained hidden for a little while, then he heard two sets of footsteps approaching. It was Lillias returning with her friend, assuring her that she had heard nothing and the whole business had been but a foolish conceit. The two girls relocked the kiln and hurried home, leaving Alastair to get out, as he had come in, by the chimney. He then made his way to the cottage where he was expected, and spent the night there.

Next day, he noticed that Lillias's manner towards him had changed. From being gentle and kind, she had become cold, aloof and bad-tempered. Evidently the prospect of being fated to marry the herd-boy was not congenial to her. In a short time, however, as the episode faded in her mind, she resumed her former pleasant ways.

15

Five years passed and Alastair grew and prospered. Now a tall, handsome youth of nineteen, he was manager of all the farm for his master. In the meantime, Lillias had rejected innumerable suitors and was still unwed. So now, sure of his position and prospects, and grown to manhood, Alastair at last paid his court to her openly. Circumstances made him an ideal suitor, but what weighed more heavily than that with Lillias was the memory of the mysterious voice in the kiln at Hallowe'en. The conviction that he was fated to be her husband made her respond the more swiftly to his wooing, so that they were married within a few weeks. When her father died some time afterwards, Alastair inherited his rich farm. And that was the foundation of the fortunes of the MacCullochs of Cromarty, a family of consequence for fully two centuries after.

DAVID PEASE

16

The Wise Laird of Culloden

There was once a Laird of Culloden who lived so peacefully and industriously, and was of so prudent a turn of mind, that people called him The Wise Laird. His time was occupied, not in vainglorious quarrels and raids against his neighbours, but in breeding a stock of fine cattle. This herd was of so exceptional a quality that many reivers longed to drive it off, but Culloden avoided all feuds and kept a secure watch over his beasts, thus affording neither pretext nor opportunity to predators.

One day, Cameron of Lochiel and some of his men visited Culloden House. In conversation with Lochiel, the Laird mentioned casually that he was afraid he would have to sell off some of his herd, since he did not have adequate pasturage. Lochiel at once saw his opportunity. He told Culloden that, unfortunately, he could not afford to buy any of these superb beasts, but he could suggest an alternative arrangement which would be to their mutual advantage: as he had more pasturage than his own cattle needed, Culloden might, for a consideration, graze his animals there. The Laird agreed, and next morning he watched Lochiel and his people drive off a score of his splendid young heifers towards Lochaber.

Needless to say, it was no part of Lochiel's plan that Culloden should ever see his heifers again; on this occasion, the Wise Laird had acted unwisely. A few months later, Lochiel sent his cousin Rory, a very personable young man who was his lieutenant, to Culloden. He explained that a band of wild Macraes had raided Lochiel's land and carried off all his cattle, including the beasts belonging to the Laird of Culloden. Lochiel was greatly grieved at his friend's loss, but his own was even greater. As the Laird listened to this tale with growing dismay, he noticed that young Rory, though apparently a very honest lad, stumbled over the answers to some of his questions and was reluctant to meet his eye. This aroused his suspicion, but he betrayed no sign of this to Rory, whom he invited to stay at Culloden. He also intimated to his family that they should be especially hospitable to the young man.

Next day, a storm blew up, so that Rory's stay was prolonged into the better part of a week. Rory himself was delighted, for he was beginning to find Culloden House quite the pleasantest place he had ever visited. Its chief attraction for him, in fact, was the Laird's eldest daughter, Jessie, a bonnie, blue-eyed girl of eighteen. In the evenings, while Culloden played his fiddle, the young people danced reels and strathspeys and love blossomed between Rory and Jessie. During the day, Rory enjoyed helping the Laird in his work and listening to his thoughtful ideas on the improvement of cattle-breeding. At the back of his mind, however, was the knowledge that he had come to this hospitable house for the purpose of deceiving his host, so that Lochiel could help himself to the Laird's heifers, entrusted to his care. Daily, Rory began to feel more uncomfortable and ashamed.

On the day of his departure, Culloden accompanied him on the first few miles of his journey, charging him with messages of friendship for Lochiel and pressing him to come back again soon. On the subject of the cattle he had lost, he confided, 'I am vexed about the loss of the beasts, too, especially as I intended them to be a dowry for Jessie; but now I shall not be able to give her anything, and I expect she will have to marry Bailie Cuthbert, the rich merchant in Inverness, who has long been seeking her for his wife. I always thought him too old, but now I expect no eligible young gentleman will take her without a tocher.' It may be surmised that this speech did nothing to soothe the already troubled conscience of young Rory.

He pondered the matter during his journey home, with the result that he arrived back in Lochaber with the firm resolve to confront his formidable chief. 'Lochiel,' he cried, on entering his presence, 'those cattle must be sent back to Culloden!'

Lochiel flushed with rage. 'Sent back! Must be! Do you say such things to my face?' he roared.

Rory then described how hospitably he had been treated at Culloden, and vowed that he could no longer be party to the deception being practised against his recent host. Lochiel refused to countenance the return of the heifers. Rory persisted, however, and threatened that, if the beasts were not surrendered, he would expose the entire ploy. He promised, though, that if the chief would give up the cattle, he would find a way of returning them without embarrassing him. At length, with great surliness, Lochiel reluctantly consented.

So, a few weeks later, Rory arrived once more at Culloden House, driving before him all of the Laird's stolen cattle. He then gave a fictitious account of how Lochiel and his people had managed to track down the Macraes, surprised them and recovered the entire herd. Culloden listened to all this with a straight face. Now Rory found himself a guest at Culloden again, on an even longer visit than before, and he bent all his energies towards wooing Jessie. It was not difficult to persuade her that he would make a better husband than an elderly, low-born merchant. So Jessie accepted him and he went to her father to ask for her hand.

The Wise Laird was considerably taken aback; it had certainly not been his intention to recover his cattle from the Camerons at the cost of losing his daughter to them instead. He asked Rory if he was able to support a wife. Rory confessed that he was poor, but pointed out that he was, after all, a gentleman and a close kinsman of Lochiel. He had a little land and a few cows, but he had never devoted much time to his property, as he had been busy fighting his chief's battles.

Culloden told him seriously that he demanded more than gentle birth and a brave sword from his daughter's husband. Seeing Rory greatly downcast at this, however, he added more kindly, 'You are both young and can afford to wait a little. Go back to Lochaber, leave off fighting and feuding, and settle down on your parcel of land. Look after your herd and, if at the end of two years you can show me a score of prime cattle, I will give you another score as Jessie's tocher.'

Rory agreed to these terms, exchanged vows of fidelity with Jessie and went home to devote himself to the task he had undertaken. He worked conscientiously on his property, improving the quality of his herd, as the Wise Laird had taught him. In fact, his virtue was rewarded sooner than expected, for, before the two years had passed, a rich, childless kinsman died, leaving his property to Rory. So it was in the splendour of his new lairdship that Rory returned to Culloden House to claim his bride. The marriage was celebrated immediately, with unprecedented hospitality and a huge number of guests. There was consolation, however, for Rory's vanquished rival, Bailie Cuthbert: most of what was needed was bought from him, so that he made a great profit out of the occasion. Rory profited too from the sound advice his father-in-law had given him, and he vastly improved the prosperity of his estates and his dependants by putting into practice all the agricultural skills he had learned from The Wise Laird of Culloden.

The Government Factor

The last of the house of Macdonald to be born in the ancient castle of Duntulm, in Skye, was Donald *a' Chogaidh*, a very popular and engaging young man. Like the rest of his family, he was an ardent Jacobite who, on the outbreak of the 'Fifteen Rebellion, marched to join the Earl of Mar. He had got no further than Perth, however, when he was struck down by an attack of paralysis which ended his active participation in the uprising. At the Battle of Sheriffmuir, therefore, his brother, William the Tutor, commanded his men.

When the rebellion failed, since it was well known that only a crippling illness, and no affection for the Hanoverian government, had prevented Donald *a' Chogaidh* from fighting at Sheriffmuir, his estates were forfeited. To administer the barony of Trotternish, the Crown appointed a government factor called Donald MacLeod, known locally as *Domhnull Mac Ruairidh Mhic Uilleim*. This Donald, a shrewd, self-seeking Whig with a fierce hatred of all things Jacobite, lived on Glenbrittle farm, in the parish of Bracadale. He was the most hated man in Trotternish and all the bards competed in composing vicious satires upon him.

Once he went to Kilmaluag, at the most northerly extremity of Skye, to collect some arrears of rent. It was here that the dilapidated old Duntulm Castle stood. One of the defaulters was a poverty-stricken widow whose husband had died the year before as the result of a fall from a rock; shortly afterwards her two sons had been drowned off Rubha Hunish (the north-western promontory) when their overloaded boat had foundered. So the wretched widow, who lived in the township of Erisko, close to Duntulm Castle, had not the wherewithal to pay her rent. Her unfortunate lot, however, aroused no compassion in the breast of Donald MacLeod, the government factor.

Having first refreshed himself at Shulista farm, the house of one Maclean a quarter of a mile away, he then proceeded to Erisko, to deal with the defaulting widow. He travelled on horseback, as befitted his factorial dignity, mounted on a small pony with a saddle made, not from leather, but of finely plaited rushes, as was frequently the case in those days. The terrified widow met him as he dismounted at the door of her cottage. Disdaining polite preliminaries, he berated the poor woman for her arrears of rent and demanded to know how many cows she owned. Weeping, she told him that she had only one. 'One cow!' roared the factor. 'Surely it is not possible that you have only one cow on this fine, broad piece of land! Come, now, tell me the truth, my good woman.'

The neighbours, who were all standing around, listening to this brutal harangue, each testified in turn that the widow truly had only one cow. MacLeod then demanded to see it. So some of the onlookers fetched the cow, which the factor duly examined. 'Very well,' he said, 'the animal is a good one. Come, lads, drive her before me to that castle there, where I will secure her, until she can be sold at the best possible price to pay so much of that improvident woman's debt to the government.'

Now, it was not to be expected that young men of Skye would relish the task of driving off a poor widow's sole means of subsistence, but, surprisingly, a number of youths volunteered with alacrity and drove the cow the six hundred yards to the castle. They were followed by the factor, leading his horse and thinking approvingly that there was hope yet of instilling the Whiggish virtues into the younger generation. Under his supervision, the lads put both the cow and MacLeod's horse into the well-fenced pasture around Duntulm Castle and secured the gate. Then, with unusual courtesy, they escorted the factor back to Shulista, where he was to dine with his friend Maclean.

No sooner had the hospitable door of Shulista closed behind Donald MacLeod, than the young men ran at full speed to the shore. From a point just opposite the islet of Tulm, close to the castle, they launched a boat and rowed round to Glumaig, a bay beside the castle rock. Within a quarter of an hour, they had the widow's cow and the factor's horse on board the boat and firmly secured. Then, with eight men rowing and the help of a sail to speed them, they set out for the uninhabited island of Fladda-chuain, about eight miles to the north-west, out in the Little Minch. They landed the two animals on the island, where there was ample pasturage, and hastened back to Skye.

In the meantime, MacLeod the factor had finished dinner and walked at a leisurely pace back to Duntulm Castle to retrieve his horse. He found the gate secured, exactly as he had left it, and the fence as impregnable as ever; but, astonishingly, both horse and cow had vanished. With the help of many inquisitive local people, he inspected the ground inch by inch, but no clue could he find to the mysterious disappearance of the animals. At that moment, the

21

obliging youths who had helped him earlier in the day arrived on the scene and joined their exclamations of bafflement to those of everyone else. Finally, one of them, helpful as ever, suggested that the only way of clearing the mystery was to consult Isobel *Nic Raonuill*, who had the second sight. At his wits' end for any other solution, the factor agreed to this expedient.

Now, the truth of the matter was that the young men realised that MacLeod's bewilderment would not cloud his judgement for ever. When he had got over his first shock, his native shrewdness would assert itself and the dogged enquiries he was bound to make might well result in his uncovering their ploy. So it was necessary to furnish him with an alternative explanation, even if it required to be a supernatural one. Isobel *Nic Raonuill* was no witch, but a good-natured, quick-witted old woman, who would help them if she could. Some of the young men went off, therefore, to fetch her from the nearby hamlet where she lived. They told her everything that had happened and asked her to invent some explanation for the animals' disappearance. She thought about it for a moment or so, then suggested it would be best to pretend that they had been stolen by the fairies, as they were known to take a kindly interest in widows. As everyone also knew, they inhabited *Tóm an t-Sian*, a mound near the castle, where they often made merry.

This plan was adopted, so the young men set about giving Isobel a more unearthly character. She was a tall, thin woman, so they placed a man's large bonnet on her head, with her hair hanging down in long, ragged locks. They put a band of scarlet cloth round her forehead and a goatskin girdle about her waist; on her feet she wore shoes that were far too large, attached at the ankles with rough calf-skin thongs. Altogether she looked as much a man as a woman, and her appearance was far from reassuring to the factor when she came clumping up to him at the gate of Duntulm.

'Woman,' he asked her, with an expression of solemnity not unmixed with alarm, 'can you by any means explain to me the disappearance of two animals from this park — a cow and a horse — while the gate and the fences around remain untouched?'

Isobel countered by enquiring whether the animals had belonged to the Chief, Donald *a' Chogaidh*. 'No, woman — if woman you be — the horse belonged to me and the cow is government property, but lately belonged to the widow of *Iain Mac Dhomhnuill Mhic Alasdair*; she gave me it this morning in lieu of arrears of rent.'

'Gave you!' snarled Isobel, in a voice of doom. 'You villain, you took the animal away! You robbed the destitute widow of her only cow — and mark the just, but terrible, retribution! Only an hour ago, I heard a dismal noise, and on casting my eyes eastward over the castle rock, I beheld a strange sight which I now, but did not then, comprehend.'

Then in the same hollow voice, and in language that was colourful in the extreme, she described how she had seen the clouds revolve like a whirlpool, out of which red flames stabbed down at the earth, with thousands of green-clad fairies swarming in these clouds. It had been obvious that the fairies were enraged by some crime that had been committed close to their dwelling-place in *Tóm an t-Sian*. While watching, she had then seen the transformed figures of a cow and a horse rising up from the earth and disappearing into the fiery, glowering clouds. Although the entire vision had lasted only five minutes, she was certain that the fairies, as the friends of all widows and orphans, had carried off the cow and the horse for safekeeping in their dwelling-place and that this was an act of justice.

The factor, for all his Whiggish views and social pretensions, was a deeply superstitious man at bottom. He trembled with fear as he listened to Isobel and his knees buckled under him. Scarcely had he the strength to totter away from Duntulm, though he made the best speed he could, on foot, and with scant dignity. Never again did he muster the courage to visit the place, so the widow was not harassed with demands for her rent: so far as Donald MacLeod was concerned, she might live rent-free for the rest of her days. She was more prosperous, anyway, for the young men who had so boldly championed her, rowed out to Fladda-chuain not long afterwards and ferried ashore the cow and the horse, both of which they presented to her. In the course of time, the barony of Trotternish was restored to the much-loved Donald *a' Chogaidh*, and the harsh reign of Donald MacLeod was no more than a scornful memory.

Menzies of Culdares

The house of Culdares was one of the principal cadets of Menzies and strongly Jacobite in sentiment. Another, less warlike, claim to fame was that the first larch saplings in Scotland were planted at Culdares. During the 'Fifteen Rebellion, James Menzies of Culdares and his brothers were 'out' for James VIII and were all taken prisoner. Culdares himself was captured at Preston and taken to London; his younger brothers were sent to Carlisle Castle.

When proceedings were taken against the Jacobite prisoners, the Crown was inclined to leniency in the cases of the two younger brothers, on the grounds of their youth and inexperience. After a few months, therefore, they were released. Culdares, of whose conduct a more serious view was taken, was sentenced to death. His young brothers resolved to rescue him, so they set out for London, dressed themselves as girls and were admitted to the prison in the guise of 'sisters' to Culdares.

Alone with him in his cell, they proposed that one of them should change clothes with the prisoner, enabling him to escape. Culdares, however, refused to hear of this. He maintained that such an action by his brothers, after the clemency shown them, would be seen as rank ingratitude. There was also the possibility that the Crown might take the life of the remaining brother in place of the one who had escaped, especially since he had so recently been charged with treason and rebellion. In these circumstances, finding their elder brother immovable, the two young men could only take a heart-broken final farewell of him.

But Culdares was not fated to die. Not long after, he received a pardon and returned to Scotland, accompanied by his brothers. He lived quietly at home, but remained a Jacobite in his heart. When Prince Charles raised his standard in 1745, however, the Laird of Culdares found himself in a dilemma. He felt that he could not, in honour, draw sword against the government which had spared his life, yet with all his heart he wished success to the Prince's desperate enterprise. So he stayed at home, though the clan joined the Jacobite army, under the leadership of Menzies of Shian.

To show where his true loyalties still lay, however, Culdares sent the Prince a present of a fine charger when he marched south. The

horse was taken to Prince Charles by a faithful servant of Culdares called John Macnaughton, from Glenlyon in Perthshire. He was taken prisoner and tried and condemned to death at Carlisle. What the authorities wanted to know was the identity of the man — obviously someone of consequence — who had sent the horse to the

Prince. So they threatened Macnaughton with instant execution if he refused to give his master's name, while offering him a pardon if he would reveal it.

The loyal servant declared stoutly that he knew what the consequences would be for his master if he were to betray him and that forfeiting his own life was nothing in comparison. Even when led out to execution, he was given a final opportunity to turn King's evidence. He asked his captors if they seriously supposed him to be such a villain. Then he told them that if he obeyed their wishes and betrayed his master he could never return home, for he would be execrated and driven out of Glenlyon. So he kept faith and lost his life, while saving that of Menzies of Culdares. The latter lived long afterwards, a typical Highland patriarch who was much respected by all who knew him. He survived for sixty years after the capital sentence passed on him at London, dying at a ripe old age in 1776.

Donald Óg Macaulay

Donald Og Macaulay, great-grandson of the celebrated Donald Càm Macaulay, was orphaned at fifteen and had to support the rest of his family by his own efforts. Despite the struggles of his early years, he grew up into a man of extraordinary size and massive strength — a giant — around whom many songs and stories were composed in the Western Isles.

Not every one of the stories told about him, however, was to his credit, for the giant had one weakness: he was a very poor swordsman. He generally contrived to conceal this defect and his great strength could usually be relied on to see him through any tussle. But the knowledge that he was unskilled with the most honourable of all weapons rankled in his mind and he became obsessed with the notion of establishing his reputation in swordsmanship. The story of how he set about doing so, and the consequences, is in sad contrast to the other feats of this Highland hero.

It happened that there lived at Berneray, in Harris, a man called Donald Roy MacLeod, a swordsman of great repute whose skill was legendary. He was getting on in years, though, and it seemed likely that his powers might be failing. It occurred to Donald Óg Macaulay that if, with the help of his great strength, he could defeat the older man, then he would gain the reputation of being the greatest swordsman in the Highlands. So he sent a challenge to MacLeod, proposing that he should meet him, with twelve men, at Tolmachan, a hamlet in Harris.

'Tell MacLeod,' he instructed his messenger, 'that I hear he is an expert swordsman and that I am determined to try his skill.'

'Tell your master,' replied MacLeod, 'that I never considered myself an adept in the handling of that weapon and that I thought, now that I am old and grey-haired, I should go down to the grave without any slight skill I may possess being called into play. But, little as my knowledge of swordsmanship is, I accept Macaulay's challenge with pleasure and will meet him at his own time and place.'

At dawn on the day of the duel, Donald Roy MacLeod and his twelve men took a boat to Rodel, whence they travelled to Torgabost, taking another boat from there to Loch *Meabhag-a-chuain*, which was close to Tolmachan. By coincidence, there lived at Torgabost a man called Angus, son of Duncan, son of Angus (*Aonghas 'ic Dhonnchaidh 'ic Aonghais*). Now, Angus was small in stature and slight of build, indeed no warrior would have willingly singled him out as an opponent in battle, for fear of seeming to seek an easy prey. For all his insignificant appearance, however, Angus was a clever and deadly swordsman, the true heir, in fact, to the reputation of Donald Roy MacLeod which Donald Óg Macaulay was vain-gloriously seeking to secure.

From his house near the shore, Angus saw Donald Roy MacLeod and his men passing, on their way to the rendezvous with Macaulay. Seeing them, Angus's heart was troubled, for he was afraid that serious harm might befall the aged champion and his loyal supporters. On an impulse, he called to his wife to put dough on the fire for a bannock, to sustain him on his journey, for he was going to Tolmachan to fight a duel for Donald Roy of Berneray. He got his sword ready so quickly that the bannock was only half baked when he stuffed it into his pocket and set out for Tolmachan.

He had to go by way of Tarbert, so that his journey was a full eighteen miles, but he strode along so swiftly that he reached the duelling-ground just behind Donald Roy MacLeod and his people. Donald Óg Macaulay, who had been first to arrive with his twelve men, narrowed his eyes when he saw Angus.

'Who is that insignificant creature who is approaching?' he asked MacLeod disdainfully.

'He will speak for himself when he comes,' replied Donald Roy, who knew Angus and surmised what he was about.

'I am your man,' Angus told Macaulay, when he came up to them a moment later. 'And I am sure I am the smallest of all the men Donald Roy brought here. The Harris motto is "The weakest to the forefront", so here I am — Guard yourself!'

Enraged by this jibe, Macaulay charged at Angus and a fierce duel ensued. At first, Angus fought defensively, simply parrying Macaulay's tremendously strong strokes. Then, seeing an opening, he cut at his opponent's face so cleanly that he shaved the whisker off his right cheek. Macaulay was maddened by this cool swordsmanship and rushed at Angus with redoubled violence. He, however, with another neat lunge, cut the button off the neck of Macaulay's shirt, to the giant's bemusement. Then, feeling that the time had come to make an end of the affair, Angus grimly warned his opponent, 'This is your last chance, Macaulay. Your head comes off at the next stroke!'

Realising that he was no match for the diminutive Harris man, Macaulay threw down his sword and acknowledged that he had been defeated. No doubt, he was wondering what treatment he might have received at the hands of the famed Donald Roy MacLeod, if this was the skill of the weakest and least significant of his followers. To the credit of the beaten giant, he made firm friends then and there with both Angus and Donald Roy, and remained on close terms with them until his death. This, unhappily, took place not long after and, predictably, was a result of the big man's ungovernable passion. Intending to journey to an island off the coast of Lewis, he gave orders for his boat to be made ready at a certain time. For some reason, his instructions were disregarded, which put him into such a rage that he suffered a fit of apoplexy and died shortly afterwards. Thus, his death was encompassed by the same flaw which had marred his character in life — a fierce, uncontainable pride. For all that, he was at heart a generous man and there were many in the West Highlands who lamented the untimely passing of Donald Og Macaulay.

A Bad Bargain

During the latter part of the nineteenth century and the early years of the twentieth — before St. Kilda was evacuated — many visitors used to go to the island to gawp at the natives and their 'primitive' way of life. The St. Kildans were quite contented with this situation, however, for the tourists bought tweeds, woollen stockings and other goods which the islanders had made.

It happened once that a woman had worked hard all winter making a length of tweed; it was a splendid bolt of cloth. An Englishwoman, reluctant to pay its true worth in cash, offered the St. Kildan 'very good payment in kind for it'. She then gave the island woman an orange in exchange for the tweed. As the islander had never seen an orange before, she was delighted with her new possession and proudly displayed it as an expensive ornament in her house.

It was not long before she realised that she had been tricked — when her bright new 'ornament' rotted away!*

---

*This little story is perhaps unusual in that, whereas the portrayal of the English visitor as cunning and untrustworthy is conventional enough, the perfidious Sassenach actually succeeds in duping the Gael, without any reprisal to retrieve Gaelic honour. Possibly this tradition originated on the mainland, or among the Hebridean islands, and reflects the superior attitude of other Highlanders towards the remote St. Kildans.

HISTORIC EVENTS

St. Fillan's Crozier

St. Fillan, one of the luminaries of the early Church in Scotland, was of royal blood, his mother, St. Kentigerna, being the daughter of the King of Leinster, in Ireland. Fillan was successively Abbot of St. Mund, on the Holy Loch, founder of a monastery at Pittenweem and later settled at Glendochart. The saint's most enduring claim to fame, however, was to have passed down to posterity a relic which became second only to the Stone of Destiny in its national significance. This was the Crozier of St. Fillan, a ceremonial pastoral staff, like an ornate shepherd's crook, the symbol of authority pertaining to bishops and mitred abbots.

St. Fillan's Crozier, also known variously as the Quigrich, Coigrich, or Cuagrich, from its Gaelic name, has long been separated from its staff. The relic consists of a silver crook, about nine inches long, encasing a smaller bronze one. There is elegant workmanship on the silver, which is ornamented with a cairngorm, an engraving of the crucifixion and a representation of a churchman, presumably St. Fillan himself.

According to tradition, St. Fillan's successor entrusted this sacred relic for safe-keeping into the hands of the first of the Dewar family who, for centuries after, became its hereditary custodians. There was an old custom of certain families in Scotland and Ireland being placed in charge of the relic of a saint, and very often some land-holding was the perquisite of this office. The Dempsters of Edzell were the hereditary ringers of St. Lawrence's bell, for which they had a farm, rent-free; similarly, land on the island of Lismore was held rent-free, on condition that the holder 'do keep and take care of the Baculus or pastoral staff of St. Maluaig', the local patron saint, and from this office the incumbent derived the title of Baron of the Bachull.

It is said that St. Fillan's Crozier was present on the battlefield of Bannockburn, as an object of veneration, to help the Scottish army to victory, but the episode was made more memorable by a further legend attaching to the Crozier. The Dewar of the day was either apprehensive that the relic might be captured by the English, or that

Bruce would retain it as his own property, so he left the Crozier at home and took only the empty case to Bruce's camp. As the troops knelt to receive Holy Communion, with the reliquary displayed in a place of honour, the case inexplicably opened, revealing the relic inside. All who witnessed it were impressed by this, but none so much as Dewar, who alone knew that the relic should not have been inside the case.

At all events, it is from the reign of King Robert the Bruce that the Crozier and its custodianship by the Dewars can be traced in well-documented history, rather than shadowy mythology. The lands of Glendochart had been held by the MacGregors, who fought against Bruce, so they were confiscated after his victory. To the Priory of Strathfillan, founded in honour of the saint, were awarded the lands of Auchtertyre, while the Dewars, as keepers of the Crozier, received those of Ewich, another portion of the MacGregor spoils. The charter confirming this was issued in 1318.

There was further confirmation of this arrangement in 1336. Then, in 1428, an inquest was held by John Spens, Bailie of Glendochart, 'regarding the authority and privileges of a certain relic of St. Fillan, commonly called the Coygerach'. The jury found in favour of the Dewars, declaring further:

> that the keeper of it should have yearly from every one in Glendochart having, or labouring, a merk land, either free or in farm, a half boll of meal, and of every one having in like manner a half merk of land, a firlot of meal; and of every one having a forty penny land, a half firlot of meal. That the office of carrying the relic had been conferred in heritage on a certain ancestor of Finlay Jore the present bearer, by the successor of St. Fillan, and that the said Finlay was the lawful heir in said office.

It was also determined that these privileges dated back to the reign of Robert the Bruce. But there were unexpected duties attached to this religious office; if any goods or cattle were stolen from anyone in Glendochart and the owner did not dare to pursue the marauders, then he should send four pence or a pair of shoes, with one night's food, to the Dewar Coigerath, who was then obliged to follow the stolen cattle, at his own expense, anywhere in Scotland. In 1487, another attempt was made to restrict the privileges of the Dewars, but James III again found in their favour:

We charge yow herefore strately and commandis that in tyme
to cum ye and ilk ane of yow redily ansuere, intend and obey to
the said Malice Doire in the peciable broiking and joising of the
said relick, and that ye nane of yow tak upon hand to compell
nor destrinze him to mak obedience nor ansuere to yow nor till
ony uthir, bot allenarly to us and oure successouris . . .

At the Reformation, the Dewars were dispossessed of their lands,
along with all the other ecclesiastical landowners, and their material
fortunes declined. They continued to pass on the hereditary custody
of the Crozier, however, despite their reduced circumstances. In
1734, Malise Dewar, the then holder of the relic, registered the
decision of James III as a probative writ in the Court of Session. A
traveller, in 1782, recorded that the Crozier was then kept by one
Dewar who was the senior representative of his line, a day labourer
in the village of Killin. Apparently it was this man's nephew who,
inheriting the keepership, later emigrated to Canada. His son, Alexander Dewar, returned the Crozier to Scotland, depositing it in the
National Museum of Antiquities in Edinburgh.

Thus, one of Scotland's most ancient and sacred relics found a
secure home. The separation of the Crozier from its hereditary
keepers, however, did not extinguish the ancient title of honour
conferred by the Scottish kings. Accordingly, on the death of the
previous holder in 1981, his brother and heir, Thomas Dewar,
assumed the title of Dewar Coigerath (The Dewar of the Crozier)
and petitioned the Lord Lyon King of Arms for formal recognition
of the succession.

The Bonnie Earl of Moray

> 'Ye Highlands and ye Lowlands,
>   Oh, where have ye been?
> They hae slain the Earl of Moray,
>   And laid him on the green.'

So runs the opening verse of one of the best-known songs in Scotland. Many people, however, are vague about the real story behind the song. In fact, the romantic verses deal with one of the most sordid murders in Scottish history.

James Stewart, the bastard son of James V by Margaret, daughter of Lord Erskine, was created Earl of Moray by his half-sister, Mary, Queen of Scots, in 1562. This was a controversial step, since the earldom of Moray had been conferred on the Earl of Huntly in 1549 and this grant had not yet been rescinded. After Huntly's fall and attainder, the Queen confirmed her half-brother in the earldom of Moray and he subsequently became Regent of Scotland, until his assassination in 1570. The loss of the rich earldom of Moray, however, had earned the Regent's line the undying enmity of the house of Huntly.

In 1580, the dead Regent's eldest daughter, Elizabeth, married James Stewart, eldest son of Lord Doune, and her husband thus became, by right of marriage, 2nd Earl of Moray. The new Earl was so outstandingly handsome and accomplished in all fashionable sports that he was known as the Bonnie Earl of Moray. As son-in-law of the murdered Regent, he commanded the support of the Presbyterian party; this religious connection, however, was a further aggravation of his feud with George, 6th Earl of Huntly, the leader of the Catholic faction.

Moray and Huntly, therefore, were religious and political opponents, but it is likely that the main underlying cause of the hatred between them was the disputed earldom of Moray. Their animosity was increased, around 1590, by Moray's interference with Huntly's legal jurisdiction. As the King's Justiciary, Huntly obtained a Royal Commission against certain individuals, who sought the protection of Moray. When Huntly and his men arrived at Darnaway Castle, Moray's stronghold, not only were they refused custody of the fugitives, but a shot fired from the castle killed a brother of Gordon of Cluny. From that moment, the quarrel with the Earl of Moray was a feud supported by the whole of Clan Gordon.

Huntly now set about persuading James VI that the Earl of Moray had been a party to the recent conspiracy of the Earl of Bothwell and he was granted a commission to arrest him and bring him to Edinburgh for trial. On 7th February 1592, Huntly set out with a strong force of cavalry — for which his clan had long been famous — to seize Moray at Donibristle House. It was about midnight when they reached Donibristle, surrounded the house and called on Moray to surrender. The Bonnie Earl defied this summons and a shot from inside the house seriously wounded one of the Gordons. Enraged by this, Huntly's men set fire to the doors in order to break into the house.

Moray's friend, Sheriff Dunbar, was with him at Donibristle that night. Generously, he told the Earl, 'Let us not stay to be buried in the flaming house. I will go out first and the Gordons, taking me for Your Lordship, will kill me, while you will escape in the confusion.'

Then Dunbar ran out through the blazing entrance and was instantly cut to pieces by the Gordons. The Earl, as anticipated, was then able to slip through the mêlée unobserved and make for the seashore. But the elaborate plumage and ornamentation on his helmet had caught fire as he plunged through the flames and this tell-tale torch acted as a beacon guiding his foes, who at once gave chase. Gordon of Buckie was the first to overtake Moray and he dealt the Earl a fatal blow. Then Huntly came up and Buckie, aware of the likely consequences of that night's work, cried out, 'By Heaven, my lord, you shall be as deep as I!'

With these words, he compelled Huntly to strike the dying man, so that he too might be fully implicated. So Huntly stabbed the Bonnie Earl in the face, to receive a last, proud reproach from his victim, 'You have spoiled a better face than your own.'

Moray's mutilated body was left on the beach and Donibristle House was abandoned to its fiery fate. Gordon of Buckie brought the news of Moray's death to Edinburgh, where it provoked the rage of the citizens. There was some ambiguity about the reaction of James VI to the outrage and there were not lacking those who accused him of conniving at the murder. One line in the old ballad suggests a possible reason for this — that the Queen had been in love

MARY LINDSAY

with Moray. This theory seems to rest only on the flimsy foundation
of a tale that, one day, James found the Earl asleep in an arbour with a
ribbon round his neck which the King himself had given to the
Queen; that James sought out his wife, but was reassured to find her
wearing his riband, so believed he had made a mistake, while in fact a
friend had warned Moray, who returned the token to the Queen just
in time.

On the day following the murder, a more formidable woman than
the Queen took a hand in events. The dead Earl's mother, Lady
Doune, arrived in a boat at Leith, bearing the bodies of Moray and
Dunbar. It was her intention to exhibit the corpses in Edinburgh, in
order to stir up indignation against the murderers. Fearing a riot,
James VI forbade this, so Lady Doune resorted to another method of
propaganda. She had a picture made of the body, luridly illustrating
her son's wounds, wrapped it in a cloth, brought it into the King's
presence and dramatically unveiled it, with loud lamentations and
cries for vengeance. Then she produced three bullets which had been
found in her son's body; one she gave to the King, the second she

37

presented to one of his courtiers and the third she kept for herself 'to be bestowed on him who should hinder justice'.

But Lady Doune was doomed to disappointment in her demands for vengeance. Joining with his fellow-Catholic, the Earl of Erroll, Huntly defeated a Protestant army of 10,000 men under the Earl of Argyll, at Glenlivet on 4th October 1594. Argyll, whose forces had been three times as large as those of Huntly and Erroll, was so humiliated by this defeat that he burst into tears. He got little consolation when he presented himself before his master, James VI. The King, though it was his own forces that had been routed, could not conceal his glee at this humbling of the proud Argyll. 'Fair fa' ye, Geordie Gordon,' he exclaimed, 'for sending him back lookin' sae like a subject!'

Shortly afterwards, Huntly wisely surrendered to the King on easy terms. He was soon restored to favour, being created Marquis of Huntly in 1599 and Lieutenant of the North a little later. Gordon of Buckie, the leading murderer, survived for nearly half a century after the events at Donibristle, though, in his old age, he professed deep remorse for his part in the tragedy. Clearly, the law inflicted no punishment on those who had butchered the Bonnie Earl of Moray.

Public opinion, however, expressed itself in the famous ballad, whose remaining verses run as follows:

> Now wae be to you, Huntly,
> And wherefore did ye sae?
> I bade you bring him wi' you,
> But forbade you him to slay.
>
> He was a braw gallant
> And he rode at the ring,
> And the Bonnie Earl of Moray,
> Oh, he micht hae been a king!
>
> He was a braw gallant
> And he rode at the gluve,
> And the Bonnie Earl of Moray,
> Oh, he was the Queen's luve!
>
> Oh, lang may his lady
> Look frae the Castle Doune,
> Ere she see the Earl of Moray
> Come sounding through the toun.

Scotland's Last Coronation

On 23rd June 1650, having cynically agreed to sign the Solemn League and Covenant, a document totally opposed to his conscience, King Charles II landed at Speymouth in an attempt to win back his father's throne. He was carried ashore by a man named Milne, whose descendants lived in Garmouth and were known ever afterwards as the 'King Milnes', in commemoration of this episode.

Charles's plan, now that the enemies of his house were divided among themselves, was to use Scots Covenanters to defeat Cromwell and his English Parliamentarians. If his father's fate was not sufficient warning, Charles had a grim reminder of the penalties of failure when he entered Aberdeen and saw the mutilated leg and foot of Montrose, executed only a month before, displayed on a pinnacle. Already, during his stay at Pitcaple House, when the sinister figure of the Marquis of Argyll sat at his left hand, a woman called the Gudewife of Glack had called out to him, 'God bless Your Majesty and send you to your ain; but they on your left hand, wha helped to tak off your father's head, if ye takna care, will tak aff yours neist!'

During the following months Charles walked a political tightrope. His Covenanting allies were defeated by Cromwell at the Battle of Dunbar, on 3rd September, but, paradoxically, this strengthened the King's position as more and more Scots looked to him as a rallying-point, rather than to their discredited Presbyterian leaders. By late winter, there were four armed camps: the Presbyterian army of about 20,000 men, uneasily supporting the King; the Western Covenanters, opposed to the King; Middleton's Highland royalist army; and Cromwell's English Parliamentarian forces occupying southern Scotland. In the meantime, the Covenanters did not cease heaping humiliations upon Charles and vilifying his father's memory, as the tyrannical price they exacted for their grudging support of his throne. The King, however, endured all this stoically, shrewd politician that he was, knowing that his position was growing stronger. Finally, he gained the recognition of his authority which was the object of his patient intriguing: the Presbyterian government appointed 1st January 1651 as the date of his Coronation at Scone.

It should be remembered that, although Edinburgh was the

capital, the old Scots monarchy had always preserved close links with the Highlands, and the most solemn of all national ceremonies, the crowning of the Kings of Scots, traditionally took place at Scone in Perthshire, at least from the time of Malcolm III. Before the Reformation, Scone had been an Augustinian monastery, and it was in its chapel that the crownings took place. The Reformers had destroyed the religious house and its site was now occupied by Scone Palace, the seat of Lord Scone. A new parish church had been built not long before, however, and it was here that Charles II was to be crowned.

The King processed from Perth to Scone in great state, surrounded by his bodyguard and the chief nobles of Scotland, with banners displayed, the whole route lined by troops. At this time, Edinburgh was actually occupied by Cromwell and his army, so that there was a justifiable fear that a sudden advance might cause the ceremony to be abandoned. On the morning of New Year's Day, dressed in a prince's robe, Charles was escorted from his bedroom in Scone Palace to the presence chamber, supported on his right by the Lord High Constable of Scotland, on his left by the Earl Marischal. There the peers and the Commissioners of Barons and Burghs presented themselves before him, and the Lord Chamberlain, Lord Angus, addressed him on their behalf:

> Sir, your good subjects desire you may be crowned as the righteous and lawful heir of the Crown of this Kingdom; that you would maintain religion as it is presently professed and established, conform to the National Covenant, and Solemn League and Covenant....

To this the King replied:

> I do esteem the affection of my good people more than the crowns of many kingdoms, and shall be ready, by God's assistance, to bestow my life in their defence, wishing to live no longer than I may see Religion and this Kingdom flourish in all happiness.

Then the peers, barons and burgesses, walking two by two in order of precedence, processed before the King to the Kirk of Scone. Immediately before Charles, four peers carried the Coronation regalia — the Honours of Scotland. The spurs were borne by the Earl of Eglinton, the Sword of State by the Earl of Rothes, the

Sceptre by the Earl of Crawford and Lindsay, and the Crown by the Marquis of Argyll, walking just in front of the King. Imposing though this spectacle was, there could be no doubt that the most impressive sight of all was Charles himself. With his fine carriage, noble features and dark, curling hair, he looked every inch a king and the cheering crowds roared their approval. Flanked by the Constable and Earl Marischal, the train of his princely mantle was carried by the heirs of four earls, the Lords Erskine, Montgomerie, Newbottle and Mauchline; six others, Lords Drummond, Carnegie, Ramsay, Johnstone, Brechin, and Yester, held a canopy of crimson velvet over him.

Inside the church a platform had been erected, four feet high and fourteen feet square, carpeted and surmounted by a second dais, two feet high, on which stood the throne. There was little likelihood of all this pomp going to Charles's head, however, for even in the midst of so much splendour, the ministers of religion were at pains to humble him. In his inordinately long sermon which opened the proceedings, Robert Douglas, Moderator of the General Assembly, explained that there would be no anointing with oil, since this was a 'Popish' practice. 'The bishops, or limbs of Antichrist, are put to the door,' he said. 'Let the anointing of kings with oil go to the door with them, and let them never come in again.'

If these were strange sentiments for a Coronation sermon, there were stranger to come. 'There are many sins upon our King and his family,' the Moderator prosed on, and he desired that 'the King may be truly humbled for his own sins and the sins of his father's house, which have been great.'

This gracious discourse was followed by prayers and the reading of the National Covenant and then the Solemn League and Covenant. After further prayers, the Moderator administered the oath to the King who, kneeling in the presence of the members of the General Assembly, raised his right hand and swore:

I, Charles, King of Great Britain, France and Ireland, do assure and declare, by my solemn oath, in the presence of Almighty God, the searcher of hearts, my allowance and approbation of the National Covenant and of the Solemn League and Covenant above written, and faithfully oblige myself to prosecute the ends thereof in my station and calling...

He then signed the parchment containing this undertaking.

41

Next, the King ascended the platform and sat on the chair of state. Then the Lord Lyon King of Arms, escorted by the High Constable and Earl Marischal, went to each of the corners of the dais in turn and proclaimed:

Sirs, I do present unto you the King, Charles, the rightful and undoubted heir of the Crown and dignity of this realm. This day is, by the Parliament of this kingdom, appointed for his Coronation; and are you willing to have him for your King, and become subject to his commandments?

At this, Charles stood up and showed himself to the people at each corner of the platform, his handsome looks and kingly bearing drawing loud cheers from the assembly, who all cried out lustily, 'God save the King, Charles the Second!'

The King was then compelled to listen to another lengthy sermon, after which he took the Coronation Oath, worded as in the time of James VI. These proceedings had already lasted a considerable time, so, in the words of a contemporary chronicler: 'This done, the King's Majesty sitteth in his chair and reposeth himself a little.'

The latter part of the ritual took a more traditional form, apart from such innovations as a layman — the Marquis of Argyll — presiding over the crowning, instead of a bishop. Charles changed his prince's mantle for the full robes of royalty, then went to the chair of state on the north side of the kirk. The Gentleman Usher, Sir William Cockburn of Langtown, brought forward the Sword of State and handed it to the Lord Lyon, who passed it to the Lord High Constable. This great officer gave the Sword into the King's hand, exhorting him with these words:

Sir, receive this kingly Sword, for the defence of the faith of Christ and protection of His Kirk and of the true religion as it is presently professed within this kingdom, and according to the National Covenant, and League and Covenant, and for executing equity and justice, and for punishment of all iniquity and injustice.

If any of the Presbyterian divines present had been of an antiquarian turn of mind, they might have appreciated the irony of consecrating this Sword of State to the defence of the Solemn League and Covenant, in view of its history: it had been presented to James IV on Easter Sunday, 1507, as a gift from Pope Julius II.

The Lord High Constable girded the King with the Sword of State; then, after he had sat down, the Earl Marischal fastened the spurs on him. While the minister prayed 'That the Lord would purge the Crown from the sins and transgressions of them that did reign before him,' the Marquis of Argyll placed the crown on Charles's head. Next, at the Lord Lyon's command, a herald called the nobles forward, in order of precedence, to swear loyalty to the King. All the people took a similar oath with their hands raised.

After this, the earls and viscounts put on their robes, the Lord Lyon similarly donning his crimson velvet mantle in place of his heraldic tabard; this latter signified that Lyon's role in the remainder of the ceremony would derive from his ancient authority as High Sennachie of the Royal Line of Scotland, rather than his relatively modern function as King of Arms. The Sword of State was returned to the Lord High Constable, to carry it unsheathed before the King, and the Earl of Crawford and Lindsay placed the sceptre in Charles's right hand. Then, at last, the King ascended to the higher dais and seated himself upon the throne of Scotland, the object of all his tortuous negotiations and intrigue during so many months.

The Moderator delivered a further exhortation on the need to observe the Covenant, and the Lord Chancellor, from the four corners of the platform, proclaimed His Majesty's free pardon to all breakers of penal statutes; this was received with shouts of 'God save the King!'

It goes without saying that, in the modest Kirk of Scone, there was room only for a very few of the thousands of people who had come to see their King crowned. Now, however, the crowds waiting outside had an opportunity to see Charles in full regalia. Escorted by the High Constable, the Earl Marischal and the Chancellor, the King came out onto a specially-erected stage outside the church and showed himself to the people. They cheered and clapped at great length, enthusiastically shouting 'God save the King!' over and over again.

When he eventually went back inside the kirk, the Lord Lyon, in accordance with an ancient custom, declaimed the genealogy of the royal house back to its founder, Fergus Mór Mac Erc. The nobility then did homage to Charles, placing their hands between his and kissing him on the left cheek.

The Moderator closed the proceedings by pronouncing the blessing, then mounted the pulpit and declared:

Ye have this day a King crowned, and entered into covenant with God and His people. Look, both King and people, that ye keep this Covenant, and beware of the breach of it.

To the dismay of those who had thought the day's sermonising over, he then added, 'And that ye may be the more careful to keep it, I will lay a few things before you.'

What he laid before the congregation was yet another denunciation of those who should break the Solemn League and Covenant. At last he had finished and Charles, taking the sceptre in his hand once more, processed from the kirk to Scone Palace with great pomp, the Sword of State borne before him. So ended the last Coronation held at Scone. Ten years later, Charles was crowned for a second time, at Westminster Abbey, with full episcopal ritual and the reality of power, having at last been restored to the throne of his ancestors. During the 'Fifteen Rebellion, the *de jure* James VIII appointed his Coronation to be held at Scone on 23rd January 1716, and some preparations were made, but the failure of the rising rendered the project abortive.

Never again did historic Scone witness the timeless sacring ceremony of Scotland's monarchs, after that turbulent, but memorable, New Year's Day of 1651, when they set the crown on the head of Charles the King.

John Mackay

John, 2nd Lord Reay and 15th Chief of Mackay was, like his father before him, a staunch royalist who fought against Cromwell. In 1654 he served in Lord Middleton's forces, in a vain attempt to restore Charles II, until he was taken prisoner at Balveny and sent to the Tolbooth in Edinburgh. Here, far from his hearth and clansmen, the Chief might have languished indefinitely and in obscurity, but for the loyalty of two individuals.

Lady Reay, his young and beautiful wife, never relaxed her efforts to have her husband released. To be near him, she took lodgings in Edinburgh and visited the Tolbooth regularly to keep Lord Reay's spirits up, telling him of the constant measures she was taking on his behalf. Edinburgh was a dangerous city for an unprotected woman, but Lady Reay was never exposed to the slightest insult or difficulty, for she was guarded by her husband's devoted clansman and namesake, John Mackay, a giant whose bare strength alone would have been sufficient to deter footpads, but who, for good measure, never ventured abroad without arming himself with a Lochaber-axe, dirk and sgian dubh. John would willingly have given his life in the service of his chief and his lady.

Eventually, by exercising all the influence at her disposal, Lady Reay managed to secure an interview with Cromwell, who was in Edinburgh at that time. When she presented herself and explained her business, the Lord Protector turned away coldly, but she fell on her knees, clinging to the skirts of his coat, and implored him to set her husband free. Cromwell was embarrassed by this scene and anxious to be quit of such an ardent supplicant, so he tried the tactics of Pontius Pilate. He explained that he was more than willing to help her husband, but Lord Reay was a state prisoner, so that only the Committee of Estates could release him from custody.

At this, Lady Reay burst into tears and redoubled her entreaties. Now, Cromwell had no intention of releasing a dangerous royalist from prison, but he also realised that he must appear to make some concession, otherwise this hysterical woman would never cease pestering him. So, with an appearance of magnanimity, he promised her that, if she could get her husband out of gaol by some means — a favour which, he repeated, was beyond his power — then he would furnish her with a document protecting Lord Reay from further arrest or persecution. He then solemnly wrote out this protection and handed it to the importunate wife, who duly thanked him.

In fact, as the Protector well knew, this paper was worthless so long as Lord Reay remained within the Tolbooth; its only value would be in preserving his liberty, should he somehow contrive to escape. This she explained to the faithful John Mackay while, carrying his Lochaber-axe as nonchalantly as a shepherd's crook, he escorted her home. To the worthy Mackay, his chief's release from the Tolbooth seemed a simple matter, as he observed to her ladyship.

'But how can it be done, John ?' she asked.

'Ach,' was the reply, 'it's easy durkin' the turnkey body inside, and the twa sentries at the door.'

Lady Reay was horrified, and forbade the shedding of blood. But the idea of a rescue was now firmly implanted in her mind, so she and her devoted servant reviewed the obstacles they would have to overcome. At the door of the Tolbooth there was a wicket, guarded by a turnkey who usually lounged there upon a bench. On the outside of the main door there were two sentries, who either paced up and down, or stood on either side of the entrance. These three men were all that stood between Lord Reay and freedom.

There were special circumstances, too, which made for favourable conditions. The turnkey was very well-disposed towards Lady Reay, because of the polite treatment he had invariably received from the beautiful noblewoman. Consequently, he never locked Lord Reay's cell while his wife was inside visiting him, and in recent days he had even taken to allowing the prisoner to accompany her ladyship as far as the wicket when she was leaving. Considering the laxity of the security, therefore, it seemed to Lady Reay that, with the help of the formidable John Mackay, a rescue was not impossible. She extracted a promise from John, however, that no one should be killed in the attempt.

Next day, Lady Reay visited her husband as usual and, at her departure, he walked with her as far as the wicket. Then, while she was passing through, he suddenly seized the turnkey, threw him down in the passage and jammed the heavy bench on top of him. It was the work of a moment to relieve the winded gaoler of his keys, dart through the wicket and lock it behind him.

Meanwhile, at the main door, having ostentatiously surrendered his arms as usual, John Mackay had spent the duration of her ladyship's visit lolling idly behind the sentries. His keen ears now picked up the muffled sounds he had been waiting for, as Lord Reay overpowered the turnkey: that was the big man's cue to play his part. Grabbing a sentry in each of his massive hands, he hurled one to the ground and threw the other on top of him. Then he kicked away the weapons they had dropped, out of their reach. At that same instant, Lord and Lady Reay ran out of the main door and, springing over the prostrate bodies of the sentries, made off down the street.

Big John Mackay thus found himself, momentarily but gloriously, in command of the Tolbooth of Edinburgh. Since he had pledged himself not to spill blood, he used other means to delay the pursuit. While the startled sentries gaped up at him from where they lay sprawled, he calmly explained that, if they tried violence against him, he would crack their heads together, but if they behaved peaceably he would give himself up. And so he did, was heavily manacled and took his chief's place as a prisoner in the Tolbooth.

Later, John Mackay was tried for assisting the escape of a state prisoner, the Lord Protector Cromwell himself presiding over the court. In his judgement, Cromwell observed that there could be no doubt that the servant had forfeited his life, but his conduct and fidelity towards his master had been such that, if he were punished for it, all faithful servants would be discouraged from doing their duty. Considering also that no real damage had been done to the interests of the state, Cromwell concluded: 'I therefore propose that, for the sake of justice, John Mackay, the prisoner at the bar, shall be condemned to death; but that, under the circumstances of the case, the punishment shall be remitted, and Mackay shall leave the bar a free man.'

So Mackay was formally condemned to death, but walked from the court, larger than life. During these proceedings, the two principal actors in the drama, Oliver Cromwell and John Mackay, had been taking stock of each other. Happily each recorded his impression. On seeing the giant's huge frame and warlike demeanour, Cromwell exclaimed, 'May I ever be kept from the devil's and that man's grasp!' Of the Lord Protector, John Mackay observed cannily, 'The deil's no' sae dour as he's ca'ed.'

A Loyal Mutiny

An incident of the Jacobite War of 1689 provided a striking illustration of just how democratic the Highland clan system could be, if a chief was really out of sympathy with his clansmen.

For reasons of policy, Lord Tullibardine, son and heir of the Marquis of Atholl, gathered a strong force of Atholl men to support the usurper William of Orange, though the feeling of the district was staunchly Jacobite. He was joined in this treachery by Hugh, Lord Lovat, the chief of Clan Fraser, who was married to Tullibardine's sister, Lady Amelia Murray, and who brought three hundred of his clansmen to the muster at Blair Castle. Since it would have been impossible to persuade the men to join the colours if they had known their true destination, their respective commanders had pretended to them that they were to fight for James VII, believing that once they were mustered under arms and subject to military discipline they would obey orders, however unpalatable.

So, when the whole force was formed up for review in front of Blair Castle, Lord Tullibardine revealed that they were to join the army of William of Orange. At this, the Frasers broke ranks and rushed to the nearby stream of Banovy, where they filled their bonnets with spring water and defiantly drank the health of King James. The rest of the Atholl men followed suit.

Then, discarding their traitorous leaders, they placed themselves under the command of the Laird of Ballechin and 'fifteen hundred of the men of Athole, as reputable for arms as any in the kingdom' marched off with colours flying and pipes playing to join the Jacobite army of Bonnie Dundee. After this democratic decision, the embarrassed Mac Shimidh had perforce to follow his own men into the Jacobite camp, thus presenting the spectacle of a great Highland chief who had been taught his duty by his clansmen.

The Appin Murder

The most notorious and controversial murder in all Scottish history was the shooting of Colin Campbell of Glenure, at Lettermore, near Ballachulish Ferry, on 14th May 1752. It was the final culmination of the bitter political and clan feuds that had bedevilled Scotland for almost a thousand years, and the widespread belief that an innocent man was hanged for the murder, sacrificed to these same historical hatreds, added to the intensity of the drama surrounding the affair.

Colin Campbell of Glenure was the eldest son of Patrick Campbell of Barcaldine and Glenure by his second wife, a Lochiel Cameron. During the 'Forty-five he fought on the Hanoverian side and after the rebellion was crushed he was appointed Crown factor, to manage several forfeited estates. Although a Whig, he had Jacobite connections on his mother's side and he was not a harsh or tyrannical man; indeed, in the hysterical atmosphere after Culloden, he was even suspected of being too indulgent towards Jacobites. Among the estates under his charge was that of Ardshiel, in Appin, to which he was appointed early in 1749.

The owner of this estate had been Charles Stewart of Ardshiel, who had commanded the Appin contingent in the Jacobite army at Culloden and who was living in exile in France. His illegitimate half-brother, James Stewart of the Glen (*Seumas a' Ghlinne*), who had also fought for Prince Charles, was still living in Appin and Glenure appeased local feeling by appointing him assistant factor. James of the Glen was thus in a position to ensure that Jacobite tenants were not evicted and that money was sent abroad to the exiled chief. At first, therefore, relations were cordial enough between Glenure and James of the Glen.

It happened that a kinsman of James, one Donald Stewart, had died and left him the charge of taking care of his children. One of these was an unruly youth called Allan Breck (meaning 'Pock-marked'), who eventually left his native Appin and enlisted in the army. During the 'Forty-five, he was taken prisoner at Prestonpans and promptly changed sides, fighting in the Jacobite army for the remainder of the campaign, after which he escaped to France. There he became a cadet in Ogilvy's Regiment, composed of exiled Scots, and he made regular secret visits to Appin to recruit his fellow clansmen into the French service, as well as acting as courier to bring money from his faithful tenants to support the fugitive Ardshiel.

In 1751, the previously harmonious relationship between Glenure and James of the Glen took a discordant turn when the factor demanded that James should give up his farm of Glenduror, at Whitsun. James did so, and went to Acharn, while Glenduror was given to another Campbell, thus fuelling the fires of clan hatred. Glenure, however, was by now anxious to clear his name of any suspicion of Jacobite sympathies which would prevent him obtaining a more lucrative government post, so he had resolved on a harsher policy towards Jacobite tenants. James of the Glen was loud in his complaints, abusing Glenure to all who would listen, notably on one occasion in an inn at Teynaluib. In April 1752, he went to Edinburgh in an effort to use legal proceedings to stop Glenure evicting tenants. On 5th May 1752, when James had already returned to Appin, his Bill of Suspension was refused by Lord Haining, so that Glenure was free to eject the Ardshiel tenants.

Appin, understandably, was by now seething with resentment against Glenure. Allan Breck Stewart was in the country, on one of his covert visits, and he was vehement in his threats against the factor, as, apparently, were the Camerons, his own maternal cousins. Glenure himself seems to have been aware of this latter threat, for, when he crossed the Ballachulish Ferry on 14th May — the fatal day — he observed with relief: 'I am safe now that I am out of my mother's country.'

The course of events on the day of the murder, Thursday, 14th May 1752, ran as follows. Colin Campbell of Glenure set out from Fort William, bound for Appin, meaning to spend the night in the inn at Kintalline and carry out the Ardshiel evictions on the following day. He was accompanied by a Sheriff-officer, his illegitimate nephew Mungo Campbell, who was a lawyer, and his servant. As they rode up from Ballachulish Ferry, past the wood of Lettermore, at about five o'clock in the evening, a shot was heard and Glenure slumped in his saddle, crying out, 'Oh, I am dead!'

Mungo Campbell then saw a man with a short, dark-coloured coat, carrying a gun, hurrying off up the hillside, but too far away to be recognisable. Two bullets had passed through Glenure, who called out to his nephew to look to his own safety. Then he fumbled at his shirt to try to look at his wounds, but died within minutes. His nephew and the Sheriff-officer stayed beside his body, sending the

JOANNA YOUNG.

servant for help. He made his way to James of the Glen at Acharn and told him what had happened. James did not himself go to the site of the murder — a circumstance that put him in a bad light later on — but the rest of the countryside flocked to Lettermore. Mungo Campbell, possibly unjustly, assumed that they had come to gloat and gave them scant civility. He took his uncle's body by boat to the inn at Kintalline and later to Glenure. On 26th May, the murdered factor was laid to rest at Ardchattan Priory, in the burial-ground of the Campbells of Barcaldine.

The general belief was that the murder had been committed by Allan Breck Stewart. Indeed, he had set out from Ballachulish, just a mile from the site of the ambush, around noon that day, allegedly to go fishing. He was seen there again at nightfall. A huge manhunt was launched to capture him, a newspaper of the time publishing the following description:

> He is about 5 feet 10 inches high; his face much marked with the small Pox, black bushy hair put up in a bag, a little in-knee'd, round shouldered, has full black eyes, and is about 30 years of age. He is dressed much like a French cadet, shabby with an inclination to be genteel.

But, though search parties scoured the West Highlands, the wily Allan Breck Stewart evaded capture and got clean away. He was last sighted at Invernahadden, in Rannoch, at the end of May, and his discarded tell-tale clothing was found in a cleft in a rock at Koalis-nacoan in July. Long after, Sir Walter Scott claimed that a friend of his had met Allan Breck in his old age, in Paris, on the eve of the French Revolution.

The escape of the principal suspect, however, was not to be allowed to frustrate the Campbells in their lust for Stewart blood. James of the Glen was arrested and charged as an accessory. Whether or not James was guilty — a question fiercely debated for centuries — what cannot be doubted is the biased nature of his trial. It began on 21st September* at Inveraray, the capital of Clan Campbell, with the Duke of Argyll, Chief of the Campbells and Lord Justice-General, as presiding judge.

Of the fifteen jurymen, eleven were Campbells. With a court so composed, the verdict was a foregone conclusion. On 25th September, James Stewart of the Glen was sentenced to be taken to Ballachulish and there to be hanged by the neck on a gibbet until dead, his body thereafter to be suspended in chains.

Throughout, the condemned man strongly protested his innocence. He was taken to Fort William to await execution and removed to Ballachulish on 7th November, the principle being that the murderer should expiate his crime close to the place where it had been committed. On 8th November 1752, he was led to Cnap

---

* On 3rd September 1752, the Old Style (Julian) Calendar was replaced in Scotland by the New Style (Gregorian). That date thus became 14th September, so that James of the Glen actually enjoyed eleven fewer days of life than would appear from a casual reading of the dates.

Chaolis Mhic Pharuig, beside Ballachulish Ferry, where a gibbet had been set up. The strong winds on the previous day had prevented the prisoner and his escort from crossing the ferry. Even now, the storm was so great that people could scarcely stand upright on the hillside. The place of execution was reached a little after midday; a small tent had been erected to accommodate the prisoner and the two ministers in attendance. After the ministers had offered a brief prayer, James of the Glen produced three copies of a speech he had prepared; one he gave to the Sheriff Substitute of Argyllshire, another to the officer commanding the troops, the third he asked permission to read aloud.

This was granted and Stewart read a long and detailed statement, controverting many points of evidence led against him at his trial.

In the penultimate paragraph he declared:

> I die an unworthy member of the Episcopal Church of Scotland, as established before the Revolution, in full charity with all mortals, sincerely praying God may bless all my friends and relations, benefactors and well-wishers, particularly my poor wife and children, who in a special manner I recommend to His divine care and protection; and may the same God pardon and forgive all that ever did or wished me evil, as I do from my heart forgive them. I die in full hopes of mercy, not through any merit in myself, as I freely own I merit no good at the hands of my offended God; but my hope is through the blood, merits, and mediation of the ever-blessed Jesus, my Redeemer and glorious Advocate, to whom I recommend my spirit. Come, Lord Jesus, come quickly.

Tradition has it that, as he mounted the scaffold, James recited the Thirty-fifth Psalm, known afterwards in that area as 'James of the Glen's Psalm' (*Salm Sheumais a' Ghlinne*). The bad weather had prolonged the proceedings, but at a little before five o'clock in the evening, James Stewart of the Glen was dead and his body hung in chains. To prevent any of his kinsmen removing the corpse for burial, fifteen soldiers were stationed at Ballachulish to guard it. In January of the following year they were still at their post and the local tenants were ordered to build a hut to provide shelter for the troops. The guard remained until April, 1754.

On 30th January 1755, the body was blown down from the gibbet; but the authorities had it reconstructed with the help of wire and re-erected it on 17th February. According to tradition, a local

53

madman — saner perhaps than those who imposed this grisly vigil — known as Macphee of the Madness (*Mac a Phi a chuthaich*), knocked down the gallows and threw it into Loch Leven; from there, it is said, it floated down to Loch Linnhe and up Loch Etive, before being washed ashore at Bonawe where it was used to supply part of a wooden bridge.

Tradition also claims that the dead man's friend, John Stewart, younger of Ballachulish, reverently removed the bones and buried them secretly at night among the remains of others of the house of Ardshiel, in Keil churchyard, in Duror of Appin.

There is one other traditional story connected with the Appin Murder. Many years after these tragic events, a girl called Janet MacInnes was looking after her father's cattle in the glen beside Ballachulish, when she found an old gun hidden inside an elder tree. She took it to old Stewart of Ballachulish, who looked it over and observed grimly: 'That is the black gun of the misfortune, Janet.' Whether this surmise was true or not, the old musket was preserved locally as an historical relic. As regards the question of who really murdered Colin Campbell of Glenure — James Stewart, Allan Breck, or some other party — it is unlikely that history will ever come to a wholly satisfactory verdict. Few people today, however, would confidently endorse that reached by a Campbell jury in Inveraray in 1752 and the monument to James of the Glen which now overlooks Ballachulish Ferry is seen by most as a memorial to a second murder — albeit judicially sanctioned — done in Appin that melancholy year.

CLAN FEUDS

The North Inch of Perth

One of the most memorable battles in Highland history was fought on the North Inch of Perth on Thursday, 28th September 1396, between the Clan Chattan and the Clan Kay*. The King had given permission for the long-standing feud between the two clans to be resolved by formal combat, in his presence, between thirty men on each side. For this purpose, a special barras, or enclosure, was built on the North Inch of Perth, between the river and the Black Friars' monastery, roughly on the site now occupied by the race-course. King Robert III, his brother the Earl of Fife, and all the court sat in a special stand erected above the lists, to watch the fight. This was no crude brawl between undisciplined clansmen, but a formal duel, officially sanctioned by the law of the land and presided over by the Earl Marischal, the Lord High Constable of Scotland and the royal heralds.

The fight was delayed by a misfortune which befell Clan Chattan: one of its thirty champions took fright and fled. At first, no substitute could be found, but eventually a Perth burgher, 'a bargaining loon of only middling stature but fierce', agreed to take the place of the man who had run off, provided he was guaranteed support for the rest of his days. According to tradition, the new-comer was by blood a member of Clan Chattan; his name was handed down to posterity as *An gobha chruim* — the Crooked Smith.

The contestants were allowed no armour and each man was identically armed with a sword, battle-axe, dirk and a bow with just three arrows. After the preliminary proclamations and ceremonies, the signal was given to begin. An arrow shot by the Crooked Smith opened the hostilities and the men attacked each other with desperate

---

* Although the identity of 'Clan Kay' has often been disputed, the likeliest explanation is that this name stood for the Camerons.

ferocity. In the words of one chronicler: 'As butchers slay bullocks in the shambles they slew each other.'

Relentlessly, Clan Chattan gained the upper hand. Their greatest strength was the Crooked Smith, who laid about him with devastating effect, but never suffered a scratch himself. Towards the end of the battle, about fifty steaming corpses lay on the North Inch, of the sixty strong men who had assembled that day. Finally, only two of Clan Kay remained alive. One of them escaped by swimming across the river, the other was captured and, according to some accounts, hanged as a vanquished traitor.

At any rate, Robert III countenanced this rough justice, and perhaps wisely. The Kings of Scots had always had difficulty in pacifying the Highlands, so that it probably seemed better to him that the most unruly elements should fight each other to a standstill, under his royal supervision, than that clan feuding and anarchy should have free rein beyond the control of the Crown. What was not in doubt was the fact that the Crooked Smith was the hero of the hour. Robert III, however, gained most from that day's bloody proceedings, for, as the chronicler already mentioned further recorded, 'Thenceforward for a long time the north was at peace, and the raids of the Caterans at an end.'

The Black Raven of Glengarry

For generations, the boundary between the lands of Macdonell of Glengarry and Mackenzie of Kintail was a twisting river* which was forever flooding its banks and changing course, sometimes to the advantage of one side, sometimes the other. The consequence was endless disputes between the two clans, in which pride invariably won the upper hand, at the expense of common sense.

Eventually, Macdonell of Glengarry demanded that the feuding be ended once and for all, by drawing a straight line between the two territories, to act as a more permanent boundary than the fluctuating course of the river. Mackenzie of Kintail, however, rejected this proposal out of hand and the two clans joined battle once more. In the fight, two of Glengarry's three sons were killed, the youngest surviving because he had been left at home on account of his youthfulness. This young lad became popularly known as the Black Raven of Glengarry.

When he had grown up, his father told him one day: 'An impertinent message has been sent to me from Kintail about the boundary, so I must respond to the challenge and muster our men, and you must come with us.'

To the chief's dismay, the Raven replied: 'If it is fighting you intend, you must do it yourself, so far as I am concerned. My two beloved brothers were killed as a result of your stupid feuds, and I should have been killed as well, if I had been old enough to be with them at the time; but as I can now appreciate how trivial the issue is, I will let you do the fighting.'

So his father had to march off to war without him.

But no sooner had the chief and his retainers disappeared from view, than the Black Raven sprang into action. Putting on his best mail-shirt, he set off by a circuitous route to get ahead of his father and the clansmen. By nightfall he was at the head of Loch Duich, where he snatched a few hours' sleep. Next morning, he dressed himself in a plaid of Mackenzie tartan and went on boldly to Eilean

---

* This would seem to be the River Ling, which flows into Loch Long and which separated Mackenzie's lands of Kintail from those of the Macdonalds of Lochalsh, absorbed by the house of Glengarry in 1527.

Donan, the great stronghold of Kintail, where the enemy were mustering to give battle.

No one paid any attention to the armed youth in a Mackenzie plaid — one among so many — and the Black Raven easily made his way in to the feast that had been prepared for the clansmen who had come from miles around. In accordance with custom, the food and drink had been set out on a long trestle table, at whose head sat the chief. As each man took his place, he stuck his dirk into the edge of the table in front of him, before seating himself. When Mackenzie of Kintail came in to join the company, the Raven said to a bystander, 'I want to sit next to Kintail.' Since this wish seemed to spring from a young warrior's enthusiasm for his chief, there was no objection to according him this honour, so he was allowed to join Mackenzie at the head of the table.

Just as he was about to sit down, however, the Raven leapt at Mackenzie, knocked him backwards onto the ground and placed his foot on his prostrate body, with the point of his dirk at his breast. Instantly, a hundred Mackenzie knives flashed menacingly, but young Glengarry warned them, 'The moment anyone comes near me, your chief is a dead man!' Then he told Mackenzie that, if he fell, it would be onto the hilt of the dirk that was at the chief's breast, so that the dead weight of his body would drive the blade into Kintail's heart. Thus, the situation was in deadlock; any attempt to overpower the Black Raven would endanger the life of the Mackenzie chief.

While the men of Kintail hesitated, the Raven went on to offer them an olive branch. 'I did not come here for war,' he assured Mackenzie, 'but for peace. Unless you agree to set aside all hatreds, and solemnly promise never to renew this feud, your life is forfeit. I need only lean on the hilt of this dirk and, whatever fate awaits me, you will have no more power to do harm.' Since he was in no position to refuse, Mackenzie of Kintail submitted to the young man's conditions and swore an oath twice on the steel of the dirk held to his breast that he would keep his promise. Then, in token of the new-found harmony between them — albeit strangely arrived at — the Raven sat at Mackenzie's table and the feast which had begun as a sustenance for war became a celebration of peace.

After the banquet was over, Kintail and his men escorted the Black Raven of Glengarry part of the way home. Not long after he had taken a cordial farewell of his former enemies, the youth met his father with the Glengarry clansmen, unaware of the new accord, marching to attack Kintail. 'Go home,' he told them, then he explained that he, by himself, had accomplished more than they had ever been able to achieve: he had ended the strife and got a promise of peace for years to come, without spilling a drop of blood. If any of his own kin did anything to rekindle the feud, he would give Mackenzie a free hand in dealing with them.

The amazement of the Macdonells at the courage and wisdom of their chief's son was shared by all who knew him. For the rest of his days he remained firm friends with Mackenzie of Kintail, and in later life the Black Raven of Glengarry came to be one of the most respected men throughout that countryside.

The Laird of Garth's Revenge

In the second half of the fifteenth century, a quarrel arose between Stewart of Garth and the Clan MacIvor, a Campbell sept living in Glenlyon. It happened that the Laird of Garth had been fostered by a woman of the Clan MacDiarmid, another Campbell sept also settled in Glenlyon, and one of her own sons was very badly treated by MacIvor. So young MacDiarmid declared that he would seek out his foster-brother, Stewart of Garth, and secure his support against the MacIvors. Taking his own natural brother with him, he set out for Garth Castle, which was about thirteen miles distant.

When MacIvor heard what was afoot, he was deeply dismayed. A foster-brother was regarded as one of the family, so he knew that the Laird of Garth, with whom he had no desire to cross swords, would be obliged to champion the MacDiarmids' cause. MacIvor's only hope was to prevent the two young men from reaching Garth Castle, so he ordered his people to pursue and cut them off.

In the desperate chase which followed, the brothers MacDiarmid fled to the banks of the River Lyon and dived into a deep pool where they hoped to be safe from pursuit. Their enemies, as they had expected, did not dare to follow them into the deep water, but they opened fire with arrows from the bank.

Unhappily, Donald MacDiarmid, the one who was foster-brother to the Laird of Garth, was fatally wounded by an arrow and drowned in the pool, which was known ever after as Donald's Pool. The surviving brother reached Garth Castle safely with news of the murder. Enraged by the death of his foster-brother, Stewart of Garth mustered his men and marched on Glenlyon. Only too well aware of his coming, MacIvor gathered his forces and confronted the invaders in the middle of the glen.

Since hope of settling the affair peacefully had not been entirely abandoned, the two chieftains met for a parley in the open ground between their respective forces. Garth was wearing a plaid which had red tartan on one side, dark-coloured tartan on the other, the dark side being outermost. Before going forward to meet MacIvor, Garth told his men that, if agreement had been reached, he would leave his plaid as it was; otherwise he would give the signal to attack by turning the red side outwards.

60

While Stewart of Garth and MacIvor were still parleying in the no-man's-land between their forces, MacIvor suddenly whistled, whereupon a number of armed men rose up from concealment in the neighbouring scrub.

'Who are they?' asked Stewart of Garth grimly. 'Why are they there?'

'They are just a herd of my roes that are frisking about the rocks,' MacIvor replied offhandedly.

'In that case,' rejoined Garth, 'it is time for me to call up my hounds.'

Then he turned out the red side of his plaid and sped nimbly back to join up with his men, who were already surging forward in response to his signal. Both sides fought fiercely, but at length the MacIvors broke and were pursued eight miles up the glen. There they turned and made a last stand, only to be overwhelmed once more with heavy losses. Altogether, the MacIvors are said to have lost a hundred and forty men that day. Those who survived fled over the mountains, their abandoned land being seized by the victorious Stewart of Garth, who was soon confirmed in his occupation by the Crown. Thus did the Laird of Garth avenge himself on the MacIvors for the murder of his foster-brother, Donald MacDiarmid.

The Fair-Haired Lady of Craignish

Campbell of Inchconnell had a blonde sister who married three husbands in succession, bore children to each and survived them all. The first of her husbands was Campbell of Craignish. When he died, she next married Macdougall of Dunollie, who was himself a widower with children by his first wife. These stepsons were anxious to possess themselves of certain title-deeds which the Fair-haired Lady held, but she cheated them of this prize by fleeing to Inchconnell and giving the precious papers to her brother for safekeeping.

When Macdougall of Dunollie died, she took as her third husband MacIvor of Lergychony, who was her former tutor and a proprietor of lesser importance, from the northern part of Craignish. But it was after her death that the Fair-haired Lady, already famous because of her escape from Dunollie, caused a greater controversy than any she had provoked in her lifetime. The problem was that the Campbells and the Macdougalls both claimed the right to bury her. The MacIvors, as the family whose name she bore at the time of her death, arguably had the best right of all, but being a small sept they did not attempt to dispute the issue with their more powerful neighbours.

So the point of contention was this: should the mortal remains of the Fair-haired Lady rest at Kilvorie, near Craignish Castle, as the Campbells insisted, or in the ancient Macdougall vault at Kilbride? This argument remained ominously unresolved when the day of the funeral dawned.

The Campbells arrived first at Lergychony, secured the coffin and were just about to hurry off with it when the Macdougalls came on the scene. Now, although determined not to give in on this point of honour, the Campbells were also anxious to avoid bloodshed, if possible. They resorted, therefore, to trickery. Since the Macdougalls had come a greater distance, from their territory in the north, the Campbells, with hypocritical hospitality, invited them to adjourn to a nearby barn where refreshments were set out for them. As soon as the weary Macdougalls had disappeared gratefully inside the barn, the Campbells picked up the coffin and made off with it as quickly as they could run. When the Macdougalls emerged from the barn and saw how they had been tricked, they were furious.

Their first instinct was to give chase, but almost at once they realised that this would be futile. By the time they caught up with the Campbells, they would be deep in their home territory of Craignish, and the Macdougall contingent numbered less than thirty. Yet they were determined to exact some kind of vengeance, to redeem their honour. So they raided the nearest land occupied by Craignish Campbells and carried off the cattle, driving their prey northwards until they came to Loch Drimnin where they rested.

However, when first the alarm was raised, a fast runner had raced to find the party of Campbells carrying the Fair-haired Lady's coffin and warn them of the Macdougall incursion. He came up with them just three miles from Lergychony, at a farm named Soraba. It happened that there was an old, disused burial-ground there, so, without further ceremony, the Campbells interred the Fair-haired Lady at Soraba, in a plot pointed out by the local people for centuries after, instead of at either Kilvorie or Kilbride. At the same time, reinforcements came flocking in from the surrounding countryside, so that the last sod was no sooner in place on the Lady's grave than the Campbells, now a very formidable force, turned north in pursuit of the Macdougalls.

The raiders, by now thinking themselves safe, were making holiday on the shore of Loch Drimnin. They had roasted some of the cattle they had stolen and, their bellies heavy with Craignish beef,

63

were playing at putting the stone when the Campbells came upon them. It was at this point that the events of that day, which so far had been at least partly comical, turned to tragedy. The enraged Campbells, in overwhelming strength, fell upon the Macdougalls and massacred them. Despite the Macdougalls' heroic resistance, very few of them escaped alive. Among the slain was a son of the Fair-haired Lady.

Yet even this catastrophe was not the end of the blood-letting. The MacIvors had been helpless, but not disinterested, onlookers at these violent proceedings. But now Young MacIvor of Lergychony had his own grievance to avenge, for he too was a son of the Fair-haired Lady and greatly embittered by the killing of his half-brother, Macdougall, at Loch Drimnin. He was resolved to take vengeance on the Campbell who had struck the fatal blow, and he knew who this was. The man in question, a weaver, lived at the nearby farm of Garbh-Shròin. Young Lergychony, however, was repeatedly baulked of his revenge by an unforeseen circumstance: he found that, despite himself, he had a kind of liking for the weaver.

In fact, outwith the heat of the battlefield, this weaver had a very obliging and good-humoured disposition. Several times MacIvor left home with the set purpose of killing him, but on each occasion he returned without fulfilling his intention, so difficult was it to quarrel with this man, face to face. Finally, feeling that this soft-heartedness was endangering his honour, MacIvor steeled himself to the firm resolution of taking the weaver's life. Grimly determined to pick a quarrel, he went once more to the weaver's house, where he found him seated at the loom, weaving the material for diced hose.

'Cut me a pair of hose off that web,' ordered MacIvor brusquely.

'With pleasure,' replied the cheerful weaver. He began to cut carefully, so as not to break up the diced pattern.

'Not there,' MacIvor objected, 'but here.' And he pointed to the centre of the dicing.

'No,' protested the weaver, proud of his craftsmanship. 'I will cut on either side of the dice, but not there.'

'Wretch!' cried MacIvor. 'I have borne with you long enough in a more important matter than this, but I will bear with you no longer.'

Then, drawing his sword, he cut off the weaver's head to avenge the death of his half-brother and vindicate his own honour. In this way, the Fair-haired Lady of Craignish, already long cold in her grave, claimed a final victim.

The Eigg Massacre

The Isle of Eigg is one of the most distinctive landmarks in the Hebridean seascape, dominated by the rocky ridge of the Sgurr, more than a thousand feet in height. In the sixteenth century, the island was inhabited by Macdonalds of Clanranald; although belonging to a branch of one of the most powerful clans in the Highlands, they became victims of an atrocity as dreadful as Glencoe, if tradition is to be believed. Yet the strange thing is that, although the tradition of this massacre is so very strong that it must surely be founded on fact, many of the details handed down are in conflict with sober history.*

The traditional tale, however, is that, one day in March, 1577, a galley manned by MacLeods from Skye put in at the Island of Big Women (as sailors called Eigg). This in itself was unfortunate, for there was already a long-standing feud between the MacLeods and the Macdonalds, concerning certain lands in Skye. So the MacLeod visitors were in an insolent and aggressive mood when they landed on Castle Island, the islet just off the south-eastern corner of Eigg. Some women were tending cattle there and the MacLeods insulted (some say even assaulted) them. Naturally, their menfolk soon came to their aid and the MacLeods were rounded up, bound and put back on board their boat, which was then set adrift. In view of what happened later, MacLeod historians have claimed that they had simply asked for food and that not only were they cast adrift, but they had their hands cut off as well.

Whatever the truth, the MacLeods survived the hazardous Hebridean seas and carried the story of their humiliation back to their kinsmen in Skye. Determined to avenge this insult to the name of MacLeod, they launched an expedition to punish the Macdonalds. Unfortunately for the people of Eigg, by the time they sighted the MacLeods' war galleys approaching the island, it was too late to send

---

* The massacre more authentically recorded in documentary evidence took place in 1588, when Sir Lachlan Maclean of Duart, with a hundred Spaniards from the Armada ship sunk in Tobermory harbour among his forces, raided Canna, Rhum, Eigg and Muck. According to a contemporary record, 'The like barbarous and shameful crueltie has sendle been herd of amangis Christeanis in ony kingdome of age...'

Understandably, MacLeod historians prefer this version of events.

LINDSAY ROBERTSON

for help from the Clanranald Macdonalds on the mainland. Since they were too few in number to resist the invaders, the only safety lay in concealment.

The best hiding-place on the island was a cavern called the Cave of St. Francis (*Uamh Fhraing*) or the Ribbed Cave. It lies on the south coast, behind a raised beach, its entrance just above high-water mark; it measures about two hundred feet long, by twenty broad, and its height inside is some seventeen feet. Into this refuge crept the islanders, said to have numbered three hundred and ninety-five. Only one old woman refused to join them and, with the stubbornness of her age and sex, retired instead to another cave in the northwestern part of the island, close to the famous Singing Sands of Eigg.

So the Macdonalds crouched, terrified, in the Ribbed Cave, praying to St. Donnan, the patron of the island, martyred by the Norsemen in 617. At first it seemed that they were safe enough, for the baffled MacLeods rampaged across the island in an orgy of destruction, but could find no trace of the Eigg folk. After many hours in their uncomfortable hiding-place, without light, water or food, the Macdonalds found themselves in a dilemma: was it safe to go outside, or were their enemies still on the island? To complicate matters further, there was snow on the ground, so that anyone emerging from the cave and then returning, even if he managed to do so unseen, would leave footprints that could lead the MacLeods to the hiding-place. The refugees hesitated for a while, but eventually the discomfort of their position overcame their caution, and they sent out a scout to spy on the raiders.

They almost timed this action perfectly — almost, but not quite. The measure of a few minutes was to mean the difference between life and death for the Macdonalds of Eigg. Their scout discovered that the MacLeods had just left the island: their galleys were only a few hundred yards from the shore. Within an hour, the people of Eigg would be safe. Taking every precaution to conceal himself, the lookout made his way back jubilantly to the cave. So careful was he that he even walked backwards, in order that his footprints in the snow would not point towards the cave, just in case the enemy landed again. Alas, so much cunning was in vain, for a sharp-eyed MacLeod on one of the departing boats noticed the scout, and the war-fleet at once put back to land.

With triumphant cries the MacLeods spilled along the shore; there were no tracks, not even backward-pointing ones, to lead them to the cave, for the scout had waded through the icy shallows on the last stage of his journey. By diligently searching every cranny in the rocks, however, the hunters soon found the Cave of St. Francis. This still presented them with a problem, for the entrance was a narrow tunnel which could only be traversed on all fours: the Macdonalds

could hold that small passage against an army, picking off their enemies one at a time.

But the MacLeods were not defeated for long. The horrified families huddled inside the cave soon heard them piling up brushwood around the entrance, and within minutes the first acrid clouds of black, suffocating smoke came billowing down the narrow tunnel.

The MacLeods spilled no blood that day on Eigg, but by the time they turned the prows of their war-galleys seaward, nearly four hundred men, women and children lay dead in the Ribbed Cave. Only one human being was left alive on the island. The MacLeods found the old woman who had hidden in the other cave near the Singing Sands, but true to their macabre policy of refusing to spill blood, they decided to spare her the sword, but starve her to death instead. They told her they would leave nothing on the island that she could eat. 'I shall not want for food,' she replied contemptuously, 'for I shall have the shellfish of Sloe, the dulce of Laig, the soft watercresses and a drink from the great well of Howlin.' It is said that, before leaving, the MacLeods ploughed up the beach at Laig, so that she could not gather the shellfish.

According to tradition, one boat-load of Macdonalds escaped the massacre, having fortuitously set off on a voyage to the Clyde before the invading force was sighted. When they returned to Eigg and found the remains of their families and friends in the Cave of St. Francis, the corpses were too far decayed to be taken out and buried. So the cave became a vast sepulchre until the middle of the nineteenth century, when the bones were finally removed and interred elsewhere, though the location remains unknown to this day.

At the time of this belated funeral, one of the melancholy details recorded was that the skeletons were huddled together in family groups. Small though the Macdonald community on Eigg may have been, Clan Donald was one of the most powerful forces in the Highlands and tradition has it that they took a heavy vengeance on the MacLeods for this atrocity. Yet, despite the many circumstantial details handed down by story-tellers, sober historical knowledge of the Eigg Massacre is strangely lacking, and oral tradition is more in conflict with academic history than is usual in Highland folklore. What is not in dispute is the atmosphere of tragedy surrounding the lonely cave where murder was done, centuries ago, on the Island of Big Women.

The Battle of Tràigh Ghruineard

The last battle to be fought on the soil of Islay was a fight between the forces of Sir Lachlan *Mór* Maclean, 14th Chief of Duart, and the Macdonalds of Islay. Although it took place in 1598, the origins of the quarrel went back to 1566. In that year, the sister of Angus Macdonald of Islay married Lachlan Maclean and her dowry was the Rhinns of Islay, the large western peninsula of the island. At this point in history, the Macdonalds of Islay, also known as Clan Donald South, were the most powerful branch of *Clann Dhòmhnuill*.

Years later, therefore, Macdonald of Islay quite arbitrarily gave the Rhinns to Brian Vicar Mackay, Recorder to the Macdonalds, as a reward for his services to the clan. This was the start of all the trouble. Maclean of Duart immediately protested, claiming the land as his wife's dowry and declaring that Macdonald had no right to dispose of the Rhinns. Prolonged debate and negotiations ensued, but Maclean could not get satisfaction, so he resolved to secure his wife's dowry by force of arms.

So he gathered his men and made ready to invade Islay. Before setting out, however, he made one final preparation: he consulted a spey wife or soothsayer.

She delivered herself of three warnings. First, on no account must he land on Islay on a Thursday; second, he was not to drink from a well called *Tobar Néill Neonaich* (Strange Neil's Well); third, and most important, it would be disastrous for him to fight on the shores of Loch Gruinard.

As ill luck would have it, stormy weather held Maclean back so that, instead of landing on Islay on a Wednesday, as he had planned, he was forced to put ashore on Thursday. Thus, he had already broken one of the spey wife's conditions for success by the time he set foot on Islay. He landed with his forces at Ardnave Point, then marched southwards towards Gruinard. Lachlan *Mór* felt hot and thirsty, so one of his men led him to a well which, he claimed, held the best water on Islay. Maclean drank eagerly and only when he had fully slaked his thirst did he discover the name of the well — *Tobar Néill Neonaich* — the very spring he had been warned to avoid. As if things were not already bad enough, when he reached Gruinard he

69

found out, after the event, that the place he had chosen to hoist his standard was precisely the spot he had been told to shun at all costs!

The auguries, therefore, looked ill for Sir Lachlan *Mór* Maclean. But in every other respect, circumstances seemed to favour him. His army was three times as large as the Macdonald forces. It was true that Macdonald expected reinforcements from Ireland, Arran and Kintyre, but as they had not arrived by the time the two armies confronted each other, Clan Donald had to fight while heavily outnumbered.

Before the battle, a dark, hunch-backed dwarf called *Dubh Sith* (the Black Elf) came and offered his services — for he was a skilled archer — to Lachlan *Mór*. It was generally believed that Dubh Sith was the son of a Shaw from Jura and a fairy woman. This ominous ancestry should have induced Maclean to respond diplomatically to the offer, but instead he repulsed the dwarf with scorn, mocking him cruelly. From that moment, the dwarf had one ambition: to kill Lachlan *Mór* Maclean. He went directly to Macdonald and offered to fight for him; here his reception was completely different and he was welcomed with open arms. James Macdonald of Islay, however, was slightly dismayed by the eagerness of Dubh Sith to kill Maclean, who was, after all, his own uncle.

But the dwarf was determined to have his revenge for the mockery he had endured in Maclean's camp. When battle was joined, he hid in a rowan tree, his bow and arrow at the ready, watching for a sight of Maclean of Duart. Presently, borne on the tide of battle, Lachlan *Mór* passed within range. Dubh Sith took careful aim, his arrow sped truly and Maclean fell dead. (There is an alternative tradition which relates that Dubh Sith was the only man on the battlefield who possessed a gun and that that is how he contrived to kill Maclean).

Lachlan *Mór's* horrified *gille* watched his master fall, then saw a Macdonald trying to wrest a gold ring from the dead chief's hand. He killed the plunderer with a stroke of his sword. The death of their chief dismayed the Macleans, but they did not immediately break. Further misfortune now befell them, however, with the belated arrival of Macdonald's reinforcements. The struggle became desperate and Macdonald, who had been gravely wounded, would also have died on the field, had it not been for the skill of *An t-Ollamh Ileach* (a doctor) who was present, tending the casualties.

*   *   *

GORDON MACNIVEN

MACLEAN'S BURIAL

There are several versions of the story of Maclean's burial, but the most popular holds that he was buried by the nurse who had fostered him. She was living in the Rhinns of Islay and when she heard that Sir Lachlan *Mór* Maclean of Duart, her foster-son, had been killed at Gruinard, she felt that she must find his body and give it decent burial. So she called to her son, Duncan, to harness the horse and the

71

two of them set off with a sledge for the battlefield. There, after much searching, they found Maclean's body and lifted it onto the sledge. Then they travelled south towards Kilchoman.

Young Duncan sat on the sledge, trying to steady the body and prevent it from falling off, while his mother led the horse. Since the road was very rough and rutted, the sledge was constantly jolted, so that Maclean's head nodded and jerked all the time. This struck Duncan as so ridiculous that he laughed aloud, whereupon his mother, enraged by his laughter, stabbed her own son to death.

Then she buried him nearby, at Carnduncan, named after him and the huge cairn which was later raised over him and is still to be seen today. That, then, is the origin of the name *Carn Dhonnchaidh* (The Cairn of Duncan).

Maclean's nurse then continued her melancholy journey south, round Loch Gorm, to Kilchoman, where she laid her foster-son to rest inside the church. When the present church was built on the old site, Lachlan *Mór's* burial place was left outside the new building.

THE MASSACRE AT KILNAVE

The slaughter did not end on the battlefield, for the Macdonalds, ruthless in victory, perpetrated a disgraceful deed. When the Macleans finally broke and fled from Gruinard, the survivors headed north, towards Ardnave Point where their ships were anchored. To their horror, they discovered that the sailors, who knew that the battle was lost, had weighed anchor and put to sea. In desperation, the Macleans sought sanctuary in the ancient chapel of Kilnave, believing that the Macdonalds would respect this holy place. Lusting for blood, however, the Macdonalds blockaded their defeated enemies inside the chapel and set fire to it. By a miracle, one Maclean, called Currie (*MacMhuirich*), managed to escape through a hole in the burning roof when the thatch collapsed.

The Macdonalds saw him leaving the building that had become his comrades' funeral-pyre and they gave chase. Currie made for the shore and plunged into the sea, intending to swim across to Nave Island. This proved impossible, so he saved his life by swimming to a large rock and clinging onto it by his fingernails alone, almost totally submerged, until danger was past. He was the sole survivor of the army that Sir Lachlan *Mór* Maclean of Duart had so proudly commanded that day on the field of *Tràigh Ghruineard*.

The Last Clan Battle

The last clan battle in Scotland was fought in 1688 between the Macdonells of Keppoch and Clan Chattan, as the result of a dispute over some land. The hill of Mulroy (*Meall Ruadh*), close by the ancient seat of Keppoch, was the site of the conflict. Mackintosh apparently had the better legal right to the disputed land, but Macdonell of Keppoch was in actual occupation and boasted that he held it by the sword.

So Mackintosh gathered more than a thousand men from among his people in Badenoch and, supported by a force of government troops under Mackenzie of Suddy, invaded Lochaber. When the two armies confronted each other on the slopes of Mulroy, the Macdonells of Keppoch made the initial charge, a traditional Highland onslaught of great ferocity, such as would later break disciplined troops at Killiecrankie and Prestonpans.

Well used to such warfare, however, and no mean fighters themselves, the Mackintoshes stood their ground stubbornly and refused to give way. A stalemate ensued for a while, with both sides suffering heavy casualties, but neither gaining the upper hand.

Then a local half-wit belonging to the Macdonell clan, known as 'The Red-haired Bo-man', swept into the thick of the struggle wielding a massive cudgel. So addled were his wits that he had no notion of what was the issue at stake; he only knew that his homeland had been invaded and his kinsfolk attacked by an alien clan. Being 'touched' in the head, he was also a stranger to fear, so that there was no subduing him. As more and more of Clan Chattan's warriors fell, vanquished by his huge club, an alarming belief gripped the Mackintoshes: they thought that the Red-haired Bo-man was possessed and they fell back in terror before him.

This slight advantage to the Macdonells was enough to turn the tide in so evenly-matched a fight. Increasingly confident of victory, they drove the demoralised Mackintoshes back down the steep banks of the Roy, where many of them died. Now that the day was won, their immediate ambition was to capture the Mackintosh banner. They were frustrated, however, by the presence of mind of the Mackintosh standard-bearer, who found a place where the Roy narrowed at a gorge; leaping across, he saved his clan's banner and, with it, some shreds of honour. The gorge was known ever after as 'Mackintosh's Leap'.

The Mackintosh himself was not so fortunate and suffered the indignity of being taken prisoner by Macdonell of Keppoch — known as Coll of the Cows.

Besides all the booty of the Mackintosh camp, the Macdonells also retained the disputed land. Shortly afterwards, James VII lost his throne and warfare in the Highlands, for the sixty years that remained of it, became a political struggle between Whig and Jacobite. It is true, of course, that clan interests and feuds often determined which side the chiefs supported in the wider, national struggle, but the Battle of Mulroy was the last overt clan conflict fought in the Highlands. In view of the irrational and extravagant nature of so many of these quarrels, it was perhaps appropriate that the deciding factor in the final clan battle should have been the intervention of a madman.

OUTLAWS

Macpherson's Farewell

James Macpherson was the bastard son of the Laird of Invereshie and a beautiful gypsy girl. It is said that the love affair between his parents began when they met at a wedding, and it seems very likely that it would be at just such a festivity that these ill-assorted partners would be thrown together. It was also inevitable that a youth whose heritage was half that of a Scots noble, half that of the wandering gypsy tribe, would grow up reckless, proud and wild. He was certainly a very handsome young boy and his father loved him dearly, openly acknowledging him as his son and rearing him in his own household.

These were the troubled times of the late seventeenth century, when wars both public and private were the common intercourse of Highland houses, so it was not to be wondered at that the Laird of Invereshie ended his days violently. A rival clan had carried off some of his cattle from Badenoch; the Laird gave chase and was killed in the ensuing skirmish.

By now, however, young James had no more need of his father's protection. He had grown into an exceptionally tall warrior, who was reckoned the best swordsman in his clan. His sword and targe, which were preserved long after his death, provided striking evidence of his unusual strength. The two-handed claymore, six feet long, had a blade almost as broad as a scythe; the targe, made of wood covered with bull's hide and studded with brass nails, was scored and pierced in many places, recalling innumerable fights.

Young James Macpherson, therefore, became a freebooter and preyed relentlessly on those whom he deemed to be the enemies of his interests and name. In doing so, he in no way betrayed the partial gentility of his birth, for, like his contemporaries, he considered warfare and plunder the only decent occupations for a Highland gentleman. It was always claimed on his behalf, though, that no wanton cruelties or atrocities disgraced his name, and that much of what he took by force from the rich he gave freely to the poor. Such sentimental stories are often made up about famous brigands, of course, and there is no means of knowing whether Macpherson deserved credit for this.

One tale of his adventures, however, does somewhat bear out this view of him as a man of conscience. The first time he fell into the clutches of the law was as a result of a quarrel with one of his followers who wanted to plunder a gentleman's house while the bodies of his wife and two children lay inside, awaiting burial. Macpherson humanely forbade this, whereupon his frustrated clansman betrayed him to the authorities. Before he could be brought to trial, the resourceful Macpherson managed to make his escape.

An ominous outcome of this episode was that the magistrates of Aberdeen now realised that the best way to capture the elusive Macpherson was by ruse and betrayal. So the cunning burghers set themselves to consider what were the weaknesses in his armour, which they might exploit to bring him within their power. Now, James Macpherson was not simply a brute with a bloodied sword and an unquenchable thirst for booty. There was another side to his character: he was a great lover of women, to whom he was irresistible, and, even more notably, a marvellous fiddler. To hear Macpherson play his exquisite music was accounted a high honour by devotees of the art.

The magistrates, therefore, took advantage of Macpherson's two great vanities, by bribing an Aberdeen girl to lure him into the city on the pretext of hearing his fine violin music.

He duly walked into the trap and found himself seized once more by the officers of the law. But the girl who had baited the trap had either been deceived herself, or was overcome by remorse, for she immediately tried to undo the damage. Knowing that Macpherson was in close alliance with a tribe of gypsies, she went at once to their chief, a notorious freebooter called Peter Brown, and told him of Macpherson's predicament. Brown gathered his men and also summoned Donald Macpherson, the prisoner's cousin, from Badenoch, to concert a rescue.

On the next market day, the band of outlaws made their way covertly into the town and converged on the gaol. A stall had been set up in front of the prison entrance, conveniently obscuring it. Donald Macpherson and Peter Brown forced the door and soon found their man, but he was heavily bound with fetters. Brown, being a gypsy, was skilled in ironmongery, so he set to demolishing the manacles, while Donald Macpherson guarded the door with drawn sword. By now, many of the folk thronging the market outside were well aware that a rescue was in progress, but being well-disposed towards James Macpherson, they helped the enterprise by crowding round the gaol entrance in feigned curiosity, but in reality with a view to obstructing the authorities if they tried to interfere.

Among the bystanders, however, was a butcher who coveted the reward he would undoubtedly receive for preventing Macpherson's escape. He climbed up onto the market stall and leapt on top of Donald Macpherson as he stood guard, felling him and knocking the breath from his body. Then ensued a fierce struggle, the two men rolling on the ground and clawing at one another so frenziedly that they tore their clothes off. The butcher, in desperation, called his dog to his assistance. With great presence of mind, Donald Macpherson snatched up his own discarded plaid and enveloped his opponent in it. The butcher's dog, misled by the alien scent, thus attacked its master and horribly savaged his thigh.

By this time, Peter Brown had succeeded in freeing James Macpherson of his fetters and brought him to the prison door. The friendly spectators threw some clothes over Donald to replace the plaid which the butcher's dog was still determinedly gnawing, and

the three fugitives took to their heels.

The Aberdeen magistrates had ordered webs from the shops to be drawn across the Gallowgate, but Donald Macpherson cut a way through with his sword. As the rescue party had taken care to have fast horses waiting in readiness, young James Macpherson was soon spurring across open country towards Badenoch, having escaped from prison for the second time in his life.

Yet it was inevitable that Macpherson's reckless temperament would eventually destroy him. Two things were his undoing: his gypsy blood and his love of women. His mother's blood ran strongly in his veins and gave him an affinity with the gypsy vagabonds who were his friends. So he fell in love with a gypsy girl and joined up with Peter Brown and his roving band. In these days, his boon companion and accomplice was one James Gordon. But, in his infatuation with the gypsy girl and the overweening confidence with which his two escapes had inspired him, Macpherson was growing careless. His bitter enemies, the Banffshire lairds on whom he had preyed for years, noticed this and, while biding their time, their hopes of recapturing him grew daily. Even the escapades in which Macpherson now involved himself were ignoble compared to his former exploits.

Finally, one day in the year 1700, he and his comrades indulged in a pointless brawl, which turned into a riot, at Keith market — a futile turmoil which did not even offer a prospect of serious booty. Here they were captured by Macpherson's old enemy, Duff of Braco. This time, the authorities were determined there should be no escape. Macpherson was held under close guard, then almost immediately brought to trial, indicted by the Procurator-Fiscal, along with his three companions, James Gordon and Peter and Donald Brown, as 'Being knoune habit and repute to be Egiptians and wagabonds, and keeping ye mercats in yr ordinaire manner of thieving and purse-cutting, or guiltie of the rest of the crimes of theft, and masterfull bangstree and oppression.'

When the accused were brought into court at Banff, the Laird of Grant protested against the proceedings, maintaining that, since they dwelt within the Regality of Grant, over which he had jurisdiction of pit and gallows, it was his right to try them. The Sheriff of Banff, however, Nicholas Dunbar of Castlefield, overruled him and ordered a jury to be empanelled the next day. Although the evidence against the accused rested more on their evil reputation than on solid facts, they were all found guilty. With indecent haste, Dunbar of Castlefield, without even pausing to pass sentence on the brothers Brown, ordered Macpherson and Gordon to be taken to the Tolbooth of Banff, and to be led thence eight days later to the gallows hill, there to be hanged by the neck until dead.

The unusually short period between sentence and execution betrays the fear of Macpherson's enemies that some intervention might save him. Dunbar of Castlefield appears either to have had a personal grudge against Macpherson or to have acted as the tool of Duff of Braco. That law and order were not the prime concern is borne out by the way in which the Browns, also grievous male-factors, were virtually forgotten and, indeed, after languishing in gaol for a year, succeeded in escaping.

Not only was public opinion on Macpherson's side; powerful influences must have exerted themselves on his behalf. For, on the day appointed for his execution, it became known to the magistrates of Banff that a reprieve was on its way by special messenger. So, to frustrate this last-minute clemency, Dunbar of Castlefield had the courier intercepted and delayed outside the town, while in the meantime he brought forward the execution by several hours. Nothing was to be allowed to save Macpherson's life.

All that was left to him was to die nobly and thus cheat his enemies of some satisfaction. When he was led to the gallows, the spectators noted with interest that he carried his fiddle with him. Not only was he a fine musician, but he was a talented composer as well, and already, years before, he had been the author of a fine pibroch that bore his name. Now he told the crowd around the gallows that, during his eight days in prison, he had composed the song that was to be his epitaph. Then he tucked his fiddle under his chin for the last time and played and sang to the hushed multitude *Macpherson's Farewell*:

> My father was a gentleman
>   Of fame and lineage high,
> Oh! mother, would you ne'er had borne
>   A wretch so doomed to die!
>   But dantonly and wantonly
>   And rantonly I'll gae,
>   I'll play a tune and dance it roun'
>   Below the gallows tree.
>
> The Laird o' Grant, with power aboon
>   The royal majesty,
> He pled fu' well for Peter Brown,
>   But let Macpherson die.
>   But dantonly and wantonly
>   And rantonly I'll gae,

79

> I'll play a tune and dance it roun'
> Below the gallows tree.

> But Braco Duff, in rage enough,
>   He first laid hands on me;
> If death did not arrest my course,
>   Avenged I should be.
>   But dantonly and wantonly
>   And rantonly I'll gae,
>   I'll play a tune and dance it roun'
>   Below the gallows tree.

> I've led a life o' meikle strife,
>   Sweet peace ne'er smiled on me;
> It grieves me sair that I maun gae
>   An' na avenged be.
>   But dantonly and wantonly
>   And rantonly I'll gae,
>   I'll play a tune and dance it roun'
>   Below the gallows tree.

When the chorus had ended after the last verse, Macpherson held up his violin and asked if there was any friend in the crowd who would accept it as a gift, on condition of playing the same tune on it at his wake. So cowed were the people by the implacable vengeance of Macpherson's enemies, that none dared publicly offer him this service. His cousin Donald was concealed among the spectators, but could not show himself. Macpherson then remarked that his fiddle had often been a great comfort to him and that it was fitting it should perish at the same time as himself. With these words, he smashed the instrument across his knee, scattered the pieces among the crowd, and launched himself off the ladder and into eternity.

Donald Macpherson managed to pick up the neck of the fiddle, which was preserved thereafter in the family of Cluny Macpherson. James Gordon was hanged at the same time and place as his companion in arms; they were the last men in Scotland to be executed under the old heritable jurisdictions. More than a hundred years later, Macpherson's grave was opened and his outsize skeleton testified to the truth of the tradition that he was of exceptional height and strength. Stories of his daring adventures were passed down from generation to generation, but his best memorial is the song he composed and played on the gallows, that memorable day in Banff, when Macpherson took his farewell.

Rob Roy

The MacGregors are one of the proudest of all Highland clans, claiming descent from King Alpin, as their motto records: 'My race is royal' (*'S Rioghal mo dhream*). In the fifteenth century, encroachment by the acquisitive Campbells robbed the MacGregors of their ancient patrimony of Glenorchy, so that, having become virtually landless, the clan turned more and more lawless. The climax to this process was the Battle of Glenfruin, in 1603, when the Gregarach won a great victory over the united forces of the Colquhouns, Buchanans and townsmen of Dumbarton. In punishment for this, the very name of MacGregor was outlawed by James VI, who forbade anyone to use that surname 'under the payne of deade.'

Despite this harsh treatment from the Stuart monarchy, the MacGregors, who now lived under a variety of aliases, fought on the Royalist side in the Wars of the Covenant, so that Charles II later abolished the laws against them.

This, however, only gave the clan a brief respite, for, in 1693, William of Orange reimposed them, as a punishment for the MacGregors' Jacobitism. But, laws or no laws, it was at this very time that the name of MacGregor became more famous — or notorious — than ever before. The cause of this notoriety was the stormy career of Scotland's most celebrated outlaw: Rob Roy MacGregor.

Born about 1671, Rob was the younger son of Lieutenant-Colonel Donald MacGregor of Glengyle, and his mother was a Campbell, a useful alliance which later afforded him the protection of the Duke of Argyll. His earliest depredation seems to have taken place in 1691, when he took part in a raid on the parish of Kippen. In his younger days, however, he was chiefly engaged in the peaceful occupation of cattle dealing, in which he apparently had a high reputation for honesty. Rob prospered and was soon able to add to the property of Inversnaid, which he already owned, the lands of Craigroyston, purchased from the Grahams of Montrose. He also became tutor to his nephew, Gregor MacGregor of Glengyle.

In fact, it was Roy Roy's connection with the house of Montrose that eventually led to his career of outlawry. It began with a business partnership. After the Treaty of Union of 1707, free trading was opened up between Scotland and England, so Rob and the Duke of Montrose entered into partnership to exploit the opportunity. Each put up 10,000 merks to buy cattle, which Rob himself drove to the English markets.

By one account, these were already glutted with Scots cattle, so that the partners incurred a loss; another version claims that Rob simply stole the money. At all events, a bitter quarrel ensued between Rob Roy and the Duke, who promptly took legal action against MacGregor. In 1712 a proclamation was published, in which all magistrates and army officers were instructed to seize Rob Roy and the money he carried.

But Montrose did not restrict his vengeance to Rob Roy's person: he took possession of his land, house and furniture at Craigroyston and drove out his wife and children to fend for themselves in abject penury. For this, Rob virtually declared war on the Duke. He settled in the country of the Campbells, his kinsmen, and from this sanctuary he carried out raids on the lands of Montrose. A score of fearless Gregarach formed his little army and their exploits became legendary. The curious thing is that, for most of his life, Rob claimed to be a staunch Jacobite, yet he lived under the protection of the Duke of Argyll, one of the chief leaders of the Hanoverian faction.

During the 1715 Rebellion, Rob Roy joined the Earl of Mar's Jacobite army, but his disgraceful conduct at the Battle of Sheriffmuir was held by many to have robbed his side of a decisive victory. He commanded the MacGregors and some Macphersons on Mar's left wing, but, when urged to charge the enemy, replied, 'If they cannot do it without me, they cannot do it with me.'

In fact, the presence of his patron, the Duke of Argyll, in the forefront of the Hanoverian army may have deterred Rob from playing an active part against him. Nevertheless, the sarcastic verse allotted to Rob in the famous song about the battle detracts considerably from his legend as a fearless rebel:

> Rob Roy he stood watch
> On a hill for to catch
>   The booty, for aught that I saw, man;
> For he ne'er advanced
> From the place he was stanced
>   Till nae mair was to do there at a', man.

So, really, Rob's only active part in the rebellion was to proclaim James VIII at Drymen and the looting of Falkland Palace in 1716.

Later that same year, having resumed his career as an outlaw, MacGregor carried out some of his most celebrated exploits. Though hunted incessantly by whole detachments of soldiers, he continued implacably to harry the estates of the Duke of Montrose. One day, when his followers were dispersed and his only companion was a man called Alexander Stewart, Rob heard that his enemy, Graham of Killearn, factor to the Duke of Montrose, was collecting rents at Chapellarroch. So they made their way to the house where Killearn had installed himself, reaching it at nightfall. Peering in at the window, they saw the factor, surrounded by tenants of Montrose, placing a money-bag filled with the day's takings inside a cupboard. By a coincidence, as he did so, he remarked that he would gladly exchange all that money for the head of Rob Roy MacGregor.

Without hesitating, as if he had a large band of men with him, Rob Roy bawled out: 'Place two men at each window, two at each corner of the house, four at each door, and let no man escape with his life!' Then he and Stewart burst into the house, a broadsword and pistol in their hands, and ordered Killearn to hand over the money. It amounted to about £300 and Rob gave the factor a receipt for it, as well as making sure that all the tenants present were given receipts for their rents. Then he coolly treated the whole company to supper, paying for it out of the Duke's rent money. Since Killearn still believed the house to be surrounded by outlaws, he had no choice but to submit. Before leaving, MacGregor extracted an oath from the factor, sworn on Stewart's dirk, that he would stay where he was and keep the others with him for a full hour after the outlaw's departure.

Not long after, Rob did something even more audacious. He kidnapped Killearn and his servants, along with more of Montrose's rents, and held them prisoner for several days on an island in Loch Katrine. The money he seized on this occasion amounted to £3,227 2s 8d Scots.

After this, the Duke himself led the hunt for Rob Roy and actually succeeded in capturing him in 1717; after three days, however, the outlaw escaped. In 1719, he played a more respectable role in the minor Jacobite rebellion of that year, fighting at the Battle of Glenshiel.

Through the mediation of the Duke of Argyll, Rob Roy's quarrel with Montrose was finally brought to a reconciliation in 1722. The years of outlawry, however, had still left MacGregor with an account to be settled with the government. Having been arrested in

1727, he was actually imprisoned on a convict ship at Gravesend, sentenced to slavery in Barbados, when a pardon arrived just in time to save him.

Thereafter, Rob lived more peaceably, at Balquhidder in Perthshire. Even so, it was not in his nature to remain completely docile and, before very long, he was involved in a feud with the Stewarts of Appin. Both they and the MacGregors claimed the farm of Invernenty, so the two clans gathered to do battle. The Stewart force of two hundred men heavily outnumbered the MacGregors, however, so Rob Roy diplomatically came to an agreement and allowed the Stewarts to keep the farm. To save his dignity, though, he engaged in a duel with broadswords against Stewart of Invernahyle; as Rob was now old and fat, Invernahyle soon drew blood from his arm, whereupon the combatants sheathed their swords, honour being satisfied.

So ended the last fight in which Rob Roy MacGregor bared steel. Its inglorious outcome was in some ways appropriate, for, despite his legendary reputation, many of the outlaw's actions had been calculated or questionable. He died in 1734, alternating on his deathbed between pious forgiveness of his enemies and continued defiance. His body lies in the small kirkyard of Balquhidder, between that of his wife and two of his sons. It is characteristic of the sometimes squalid, sometimes heroic, nature of the MacGregor legend that one of those sons was hanged in 1754 for carrying off and marrying, against her will, a widow from Balfron.

MacCuil of Glenfhiodhag

During the first half of the eighteenth century there lived in Glenfhiodhag, in Argyllshire, a freebooter named MacCuil. He was a
substantial tenant of one of the cadets of the house of Argyll, but,
besides farming the entire glen, his income was greatly augmented
by cattle-reiving. In temperament he was incurably arrogant, and
he affected the airs of a great chief, living luxuriously and behaving
towards everyone with a degree of condescension which would have
been ridiculous, had he not been widely feared for his strength and
violence.

Eventually, MacCuil decided that it was time he took a wife, and
his best prospect seemed to be one of the three daughters of Fraser of
Belladrum. So he set out for the Aird, to acquaint the Laird of
Belladrum with the honour that was about to befall his house. For his
wooing expedition, MacCuil dressed himself in his best finery as a
Highland gentleman and, armed to the teeth with musket, pistols,
broadsword, dirk and sgian dhu, set out on his journey. He travelled
on foot, with his dog at his side. At sunset on the first day of his
journey, he came across a lonely cottage and swaggered across the
threshold, without troubling to ask permission. The only occupant
was an old weaver, a bachelor, who was busy at his loom. MacCuil
announced grandly, 'I have come here to stay for the night.'

'I never allow anyone to stay under my roof without first asking
leave,' replied the weaver.

'I am remaining, whether you allow me or not,' MacCuil declared.

'We shall see,' said the weaver, rising purposefully from his loom.

Thereupon he set about throwing MacCuil out of his house.
Though he was older, he was wiry and strong, and the arrogant
reiver soon regretted having taken him on in a wrestling bout. The
tide of battle ebbed and flowed, but at last the great MacCuil was sent
hurtling across the threshold, bested by the weaver. Then, humiliated by his defeat, MacCuil humbly begged lodging for the night.
This was at once generously granted. The weaver supplied the best
fare that his house could provide, and by the time MacCuil took his
leave next morning, the two men had become firm friends.

When MacCuil finally arrived at his destination in the Aird, he
found the Laird of Belladrum and all his people gathered at the local

mill for an important event: a new millstone was being installed. The stone was too heavy for the men to raise and put in place, though they tried to tackle it from various angles. MacCuil stepped forward and, with his customary self-confidence, ordered everyone else to stand aside, as he alone would set the stone in place. He stood it upon its edge, crouched down beside it, rested it on his back, then placed his hands under it. To the astonishment of the onlookers, he succeeded in shifting the millstone into its proper position. This achievement restored his pride, somewhat ruffled by his encounter with the weaver.

Fraser of Belladrum thanked MacCuil for his help and invited him to dinner. As they sat at table, one of Belladrum's servants came in to say that MacCuil's dog must be ill, as it would not eat the meat set before it. MacCuil asked what kind of food had been given to his dog and, on discovering it was offal, explained that the pampered animal was accustomed only to the best meat. Before going to bed, he revealed to Fraser of Belladrum and his lady that the object of his visit was to marry one of their daughters. The parents replied that the girls must decide for themselves; MacCuil could speak to them the next day, and if one of them was willing, no obstacle would be placed in his path.

Next day, while the Laird and his wife were away from home, MacCuil approached the eldest daughter and asked her, 'Will you marry me?'

'No,' she replied.

'If you won't,' said MacCuil haughtily, 'then I won't marry you.'

He then proposed to the second daughter and was rejected in identical terms. Then he put the question to the youngest girl, 'Will you marry me?'

'Yes.'

'If you will marry me,' said MacCuil graciously, 'then I will marry you.'

So MacCuil married the youngest daughter of Fraser of Belladrum and brought her back to Glenfhiodhag. She could not at first adjust to the housekeeping style preferred there. MacCuil disagreed with her way of spooning out the butter, so he took her to the larder, which was stored full of butter-dishes, one for each day of the year and each containing a Highland stone of butter. He opened one and quartered the butter with his sgian; then he instructed his wife to place a quarter on the table every morning for breakfast and to give all that was left over to the servants and dogs.

After some years, MacCuil was served notice that his rent had been raised. This seemed exorbitant to him, so, every rent day, he presented himself before the factor with a sum of money equivalent to the old rent. This the factor, in accordance with his instructions, refused to accept. So MacCuil would then replace it in his sporran with an indignant air and return home. After several years of this, his debt was considerable and the local laird, one Campbell, determined to recover his rents. After obtaining warrants and a force of constables, the laird and his wife set out to secure MacCuil.

The wily cateran was well aware of their movements and tracked the law officers on horseback. It happened that the river was in spate, so that Campbell and his party could not cross without boats. They halted on the bank and MacCuil grasped his opportunity. Spurring his horse into the swirling stream, he crossed the river, seized Mrs.

Campbell, the laird's wife, placed her on the saddle before him and carried her off to his house as a hostage.

In Glenfhiodhag, Mrs. Campbell was relieved to find that she was treated as an honoured guest and that every comfort was available to her. MacCuil's wife, a gentlewoman herself, proved an attentive and congenial hostess, so that the two ladies became close friends. At the end of six weeks, when the weather had abated and the river was fordable, Mrs. Campbell was released and returned home. She impressed her husband so much with her description of the courteous treatment she had received, that he gave up the legal proceedings and allowed MacCuil to hold his farm at the former rent.

But Campbell had another, more self-interested, reason for cultivating MacCuil. He was determined to put down all the outlaws of the locality and, on the principle of setting a thief to catch a thief, proposed to MacCuil that he should undertake this work, offering a price on the head of each of the reivers.

Without a qualm, MacCuil accepted this offer. The most important of the outlaws was called MacThearlich, a man well known to MacCuil who sought him out at his home at Inverlochy. MacThearlich received him with great hospitality, but, while they were talking together in the friendliest possible way, MacCuil treacherously drew a dirk and stabbed his host to death. He then succeeded in making his escape.

This outrage, however, brought about the downfall of MacCuil and his family. They were shunned and execrated by all the countryside and no one would have dealings with them. Their fortunes decayed and eventually MacCuil's children found themselves in dire poverty. Within a generation, they lost the barbaric splendour that had once attached to them and degenerated into the lowest kind of sheep-stealers, several being hanged for this offence. They were still of exceptional physical strength, though, and it was related of one of MacCuil's daughters that she could pick up a large species of snake — now extinct — and shake it by the tail until its innards came out of its mouth. This was the last, tawdry fame that the family was fated to enjoy and, very soon after, the world had almost forgotten the name of MacCuil of Glenfhiodhag.

The Big Sergeant

John *Dhu* Cameron served as a sergeant in the French army, earning the nickname of the Sergeant *Mór* by reason of his great size. He returned to Scotland in 1745 to fight for Prince Charles Edward and was a fugitive after Culloden. Soon he became leader of a band of outlaws who moved through the highlands of Perthshire, Inverness-shire and Argyll, plundering as they went. But the Big Sergeant was a man of principle and, even as Whiggish lairds feared his depredations, oppressed Jacobites could rely on his protection and some provender for their empty larders. People along the Highland frontier paid him blackmail to keep their property safe.

Once, in the mountains of Lochaber, he met an officer from the Fort William garrison who confessed he had lost his way. He volunteered the additional information that, as he was carrying a large sum of money for the garrison, he was afraid of encountering the Big Sergeant: would this Highland stranger, therefore, do him the favour of keeping him company? John *Dhu* courteously agreed and the two men walked on together. As the miles went by, the officer waxed eloquent on the subject of the Sergeant *Mór*, calling him a robber and a murderer.

'Stop there!' cried his companion. 'He does indeed lift the cattle of the Whigs and you Sassanachs, but neither he nor his followers ever shed innocent blood — except once,' he added incautiously, 'I was unlucky at Braemar, when a man was killed. But I immediately ordered the spoil to be abandoned and left to the owners, retreating as fast as we could after such a misfortune.

'You!' exclaimed the officer suspiciously. 'What had you to do with the affair?'

'I am John *Dhu* Cameron,' was the reply. 'I am the Big Sergeant. There is the road to Inverlochy, you cannot now mistake it. You and your money are safe. Tell your governor to send a more wary messenger for his gold. Tell him also that, although an outlaw and forced to live off the public, I am a soldier as well as himself and would disdain taking his gold from a defenceless man who confided in me.'

The officer made off as fast as he could to rejoin the garrison, where he narrated this adventure many times. Not long afterwards, Cameron slept in a barn at Dunan farm, in Rannoch, a sanctuary he had used often before. On this night, however, he was betrayed by the farmer who sent word of his presence to Lieutenant (later Sir Hector) Munro, who was stationed with his troops two miles away. As an added precaution, the treacherous farmer removed Cameron's weapons while he slept. He was still asleep when the soldiers burst into the barn and seized him. Such was his strength that he was able to shake them off and escape from the barn, but the troops outside managed to overpower him, even though he injured one of them quite severely.

The Big Sergeant was taken to Perth, where he was tried before the Court of Justiciary for the murder at Braemar, as well as assorted thefts and cattle-raids, including the lifting of two rams from the Duke of Atholl's park at Blair, on the retreat from Braemar. After sentence of death had been passed on Cameron, the Doomster was called into court, in accordance with custom, to place his hand formally on the head of the condemned man, as a symbol that he was thenceforth under his care.

'Keep the caitiff off! Let him not touch me!' roared Cameron when the Doomster approached him. Then he raised his great arms so menacingly that the Doomster, overcome by fear, slunk out of the court-room without carrying out the customary ceremony. The remainder of the ritual of justice was inexorably performed, however, and John *Dhu* Cameron, the Big Sergeant, was executed at Perth on 23rd November 1753, and his body hung in chains.

BONNIE PRINCE CHARLIE

The Rout of Moy

Aeneas Mackintosh, 22nd Chief of Mackintosh and 23rd Captain of Clan Chattan, was an officer in the Black Watch when the 'Forty-five Rebellion broke out. Although his sympathies were Jacobite, therefore, he felt that his honour would not permit him to break his oath of loyalty to King George. No such scruple troubled his wife, however, who was one of the most ardent Jacobites in Scotland. This lady, a daughter of Farquharson of Invercauld, donned military costume and raised a regiment for the Prince from the menfolk of Clan Chattan. Under the command of the giant Alexander Mac-Gillivray of Dunmaglass, it later fought at Culloden. Because of her military enthusiasm, the beautiful Lady Mackintosh was nicknamed 'Colonel Anne'.

On 16th February 1746, Prince Charlie himself was a guest at Moy Hall, in Strathdearn, the seat of Mackintosh. News of this visit was brought to the Earl of Loudoun, whose Hanoverian troops were occupying Inverness, just twelve miles away. So they decided to march on Moy Hall and end the rebellion at a stroke, by seizing the Prince. As they discussed their plans at breakfast, however, they were overheard by the girl who waited at table, and she, barefoot and bare-headed, ran all the way to Moy to warn of the Prince's danger.

The news was received with acute alarm, for there were no Jacobite forces at Moy capable of repelling Loudoun's militia, which some estimates put at as much as 1,500 men. But there was one brave soul at Moy who was not at all dismayed. Donald Fraser, the blacksmith, assembled a group of just four men and, helping themselves to swords and muskets from Mackintosh's armoury, they set out cheerfully to deal with the approaching enemy. At nightfall they came to the narrow pass two miles away, called Craig an Eoin, and there they set up an ambush for the Hanoverians.

Useful for their purpose were the stacks of peat piled at the side of the pass. Donald and his men dispersed themselves at intervals of several hundred yards, crouched behind the peat-stacks, and lay silently waiting for Loudoun's men. The advent of nightfall had by now made the pass pitch-black. Soon the uncertain tramp of many feet warned them that the enemy were at hand. Donald Fraser waited until the vanguard was within a hundred yards of his own hiding-place, then he started up and shouted to imaginary units under his command, 'The Mackintoshes, the MacGillivrays, the MacBains to form the centre instantly!'

The startled Hanoverians, who had heard this shout of command, halted in their tracks. At the same moment the further order rang out, 'The Macdonalds to the right, the Frasers on the left!' Then the darkness was stabbed by irregular flashes of musketry; a piper in the front rank of the militia fell to the ground. The shots came closer, as did the confused shouting of warcries of half a dozen clans. Unnerved by this ambush in a dark and lonely mountain pass, and believing that the whole Jacobite army was falling upon them, Loudoun's men broke and ran back to Inverness. So great was their terror and so firm their conviction that Prince Charles was pursuing them with all his forces, that they did not stop at Inverness, but soon retired even further north.

This easy victory for the Jacobites became known as the Rout of Moy. The piper who had been killed with the Hanoverian forces was the celebrated Donald Ban MacCrimmon; Fraser the blacksmith took his dirk as a trophy and was himself known ever afterwards as the Captain of the Five, in memory of this exploit. He fought well at Culloden and his sword was preserved as a memento at nearby Tomatin House.

Prince Charlie's Double

Roderick Mackenzie, the son of an Edinburgh goldsmith, was an enthusiastic adherent of the House of Stuart who fought with the Jacobite army. Unlike most of his comrades, however, his services to the Prince did not end with the Battle of Culloden. For Roderick had a strong resemblance to Prince Charlie, of which he was very proud; in defeat, however, this fortuitous likeness became more than an empty vanity and was put to very practical use by the young man.

After Culloden, the Prince's pursuers were hot on his heels, spurred on by the enormous reward of £30,000 on his head. Mackenzie made it his business to keep track of the royal fugitive and follow a parallel course through the Highlands. On several occasions, when the hunters were drawing dangerously close to their quarry, Mackenzie deliberately showed himself nearby and drew off the Redcoats on a false scent. He was so much at home in the hills and glens, heather and bog, that he managed to give the enemy the slip each time, only to surface again when danger once more threatened the Prince.

This perilous game, of course, could only be played for so long. One day, Mackenzie blundered into a party of soldiers who took him by surprise. He tried to escape, but found himself cut off. So he defended himself desperately against hopeless odds until a shot brought him down, mortally wounded. Even in his extremity, however, the young man contrived to serve his purpose. 'Ah, villains!' he cried. 'You have slain your Prince!'

This lie, told for the noblest of motives by a dying man, was very effective. The Hanoverians were convinced that they had killed Prince Charlie; they cut off Mackenzie's head and displayed it as that of the Young Pretender. As the news spread, the search for the Prince slackened off, since the pursuers believed that the reward had already been secured. By the time the mistake was discovered, the fugitive's trail was so much colder and the Whigs began to despair of ever taking him. It was a striking testimony to the devotion inspired by the Prince that one of his followers should not only have put his life unnecessarily at risk to protect him, but should have pursued this purpose so stubbornly, even in his dying moments.

The Men of Glenmoriston

On 24th July 1746, Bonnie Prince Charlie, hunted and very near the end of his resources, came into the care of the celebrated Seven Men of Glenmoriston; despite their traditional title, there were in fact eight of them. These men are usually described as 'robbers', yet they protected, of their own free will, a fugitive with a price of £30,000 on his head! The names of these loyal men were John and Alexander Macdonald; the three Chisholm brothers, Alexander, Donald and Hugh; Patrick Grant; Gregor MacGregor and Hugh Macmillan.

They welcomed the Prince to their home, a cave in Glen Moriston, and swore a fierce oath 'That their backs should be to God and their faces to the Devil; that all the curses the Scriptures did pronounce might come upon them and all their posterity if they did not stand firm to help the Prince in the greatest dangers ...' So the exhausted Prince was able to get some rest. A fresh stream ran through the cave, and he and his companions were, in the words of one of them, 'as comfortably lodged as we had been in a Royal pallace'. The fugitives stayed in the cave for three days and nights, with no shortage of food.

On 28th July, they moved on to another cave at Coire Mheadhoin, two miles away. Four days later, feeling themselves threatened by the arrival in the neighbourhood of an officer known as the Black Campbell, with a force of militia, they decamped northwards, to Strathglass. There they learned that a French ship had called at Poolewe, but had put to sea again. So the fugitives turned back south and made their way, in great discomfort, to Lock Arkaig, which they reached in mid-August.

The Prince lingered in Lochiel's country, trying to arrange a meeting with the Cameron chief. An eye-witness described the Prince at this time:

> He was then bare-footed, had an old black kilt coat on, a plaid, philabeg and waistcoat, a dirty shirt and a long red beard, a gun in his hand, a pistol and durk by his side. He was very cheerful and in good health, and, in my opinion, fatter than when he was at Inverness.

The eight men of Glenmoriston spoke in Gaelic, so that one of the

Prince's other followers, Macdonald of Glenaladale, had to act as interpreter. On one occasion, terrified that the Prince's imprudence might lead to his capture, these kindly brigands actually threatened to tie him up, rather than let him blunder into danger. The Prince submitted good-naturedly to this tyranny, observing, 'I find kings and princes must be ruled by their privy council, but I believe there is not in all the world a more absolute privy council than what I have at present'. On 26th August, the Prince parted company with these gallant supporters, apart from Patrick Grant whom he ordered to stay with him until he should be able to borrow some money to reward the eight stalwarts. At the Prince's request, Macdonald of Lochgarry later provided twenty-four guineas for this purpose (three guineas each); the reward of infamy would have been £30,000.

A Royal Peat-Gatherer

When the Prince was a fugitive in the Highlands, he sometimes dressed as a woman and shared in the work of the people around him. One day, in this disguise, he was helping to pick peat. While he was hard at work, a group of Hanoverian sympathisers passed by and stared suspiciously at the very ungainly woman, whose true identity was not hard to guess.

'Aha!' said one. 'The peat-gatherers have seen another day.' (*Bha latha eile aig luchd-buain na mòine*).

This saying has been passed down as a Gaelic proverb to describe people who have known better days.

The Culloden Bagpipes

In 1822, during the visit of King George IV to Edinburgh, one of the most colourful and imposing sights in the capital was the celebrated piper, John MacGregor. He marched at the head of his clan and played the pibroch *'Thàin' na Griogairich'* when his Chief escorted the Honours of Scotland from Edinburgh Castle to Holyrood Palace. He had been successively piper to the Duke of Atholl, Farquharson of Monaltrie and Farquharson of Finzean. At the Eglinton Tournament, that romantic revival of medieval chivalry which took place in 1839, he was piper to the Atholl Highlanders, the Duke of Atholl's private army and the only surviving unit of the Jacobite forces of 1745. He also had the crowning honour of performing before Queen Victoria at Taymouth Castle.

In his old age, living at Druimcharry, in Fortingall parish, John found himself in very straitened circumstances. To relieve his poverty, he reluctantly resolved to sell his bagpipes. It was then that their full history became known. There were several silver plates on the chanter, one of which, affixed in 1846, recorded the fact that this historic, two-drone instrument (as the older ones were) had been played by his grandfather and namesake in Prince Charles Edward's army during the 'Forty-five. An advertisement was placed in the newspapers, and public interest was aroused in the story of this fascinating relic.

The owner's grandfather, it transpired, also called John Mac-Gregor and likewise a native of Fortingall, in Perthshire, was a handsome, athletic man, about six feet tall. An enthusiastic Jacobite, on the raising of the standard he joined the Highland muster at Glenfinnan. He soon drew himself to the attention of the Prince and became his personal piper, following him everywhere. Prince Charlie had a great affection for his piper, and spoke to him very familiarly. There was, however, one drawback: the Prince had little enough Gaelic, MacGregor had very little English. So the Prince learned the single phrase 'Blow up your pipe, John!' (*'Seid suas do phiob, Iain!'*) which enabled him to convey the most necessary command to MacGregor. It was an order he loved to call out, doing so notably at his triumphant entry into Edinburgh, after the breaking of Cope's army at Prestonpans, and on the field of Culloden itself.

—Y·CHRISTIE

The evening of that tragic day was the last time that MacGregor set
eyes on his Prince. It was only by good luck that the piper himself
survived the battle. A ball lodged in his left thigh, causing severe loss
of blood, but he was fortunate enough to encounter a surgeon who
dressed it for him and possibly saved his life. After many hardships
and narrow escapes, he reached his home at Fortingall, where he
passed the rest of his days uneventfully. All of his four sons and eight
grandsons were pipers, the last survivor being his namesake who
offered the pipes for sale.

Several lairds made bids for the Culloden Bagpipes, but, appro-
priately, the successful offer was that of the Duke of Atholl. Not
only did he undertake to match whichever rival bid should be the
highest, but he also settled a half-yearly pension on the old piper,
which enabled him to enjoy security in his declining years. Thus, the
pipes that had shrilled out the last defiance of the House of Stuart on
Culloden Moor found safe keeping in one of Scotland's leading
Jacobite families.

The Last of the Stuarts

Dunkeld Cathedral is one of the most impressive ruins in Scotland. Behind it frown dark, tree-shrouded crags; in front, a smiling green meadow leads down to the River Tay. This Atholl country of Perthshire is, in any case, an outstandingly beautiful part of the Highlands, but the ancient Cathedral Kirk of St. Columba adds its own special atmosphere, like a jewel in a rich setting. Dunkeld is among the great religious shrines of Scotland. For a time, its Abbot was head of the Pictish Church and guardian of the sacred relics of St. Columba. These consisted of the saint's bones, his books, staff and stone pillow. At the Reformation, the Catholic clergy spirited away what remained of the relics to Ireland, to save them from destruction.

The ruined Cathedral, however, still holds some more profane remains. On top of an elaborate stone sarcophagus lies the effigy of a knight in armour, his feet resting on a lion. This is the tomb of Alexander, Earl of Buchan, younger brother of King Robert III, better known as 'The Wolf of Badenoch'. Among his terrible deeds was the destruction of Elgin Cathedral, but, although excommunicated by the Church, he received absolution before his death in 1394 and was given Christian burial at Dunkeld. In the grass-grown nave is the gravestone of Colonel Cleland, the twenty-eight-year-old leader of the Cameronians, killed defending Dunkeld against the Jacobites after the Battle of Killiecrankie in 1689. The Jacobites were repulsed, but the town was burned in the struggle, only three houses surviving. Most visitors pause to examine these two very different tombs; but few spare so much as a glance for a third gravestone nearby which, despite its modest appearance, conceals a stranger and more poignant story than either. It is a flat stone of pink marble, under the most westerly arch bounding the ruined nave from its south aisle. The mysterious inscription, rather faded, reads:

SACRED

TO THE MEMORY OF

GENERAL

CHARLES EDWARD STUART

COUNT ROEHENSTART

WHO DIED AT DUNKELD
ON THE 28TH OCTOBER 1854
AGED 73 YEARS

SIC TRANSIT GLORIA MUNDI

Occasionally a stranger, more observant than most, will stop and wrinkle his brow over this legend. Who was General Charles Edward Stuart, Count Roehenstart? Was he some distinguished Scottish soldier? Why did he bear the most famous name in Scotland, along with a foreign-sounding title? Or was he simply some adventurer or eccentric who posed as a nobleman? The true explanation is more curious than any speculation.

One day, in late October 1854, the stagecoach from Inverness to Edinburgh met with a serious accident just outside the little village of Inver, about a mile south-west of Dunkeld. A wheel came off and the coach overturned, so that a party of gentlemen travelling as outside passengers on the roof were thrown off, receiving various degrees of injury. The accident caused a stir in the sleepy clachan of Inver, so that the people rushed from their cottages to see what had happened, and women from the village did what they could to tend to the injured passengers. The most badly hurt was a man aged about seventy, small in stature, with grey hair, blue eyes and a ruddy complexion to his oval-shaped face. He was carried to the Athole Arms Hotel in Dunkeld and even in his distressed condition everyone was struck by his charm and beautiful manners. This air of distinction was explained when the local people learned that the injured traveller was a nobleman named Count Roehenstart, who had been returning from Inverness with some friends, after visiting Lord Lovat.

The satisfaction that the folk of Inver felt at having the dullness of their routine interrupted not only by a stagecoach accident, but by the dramatic appearance in their midst of a noble stranger, was soon increased by an act of generosity on the part of the invalid. Over the next few days, Count Roehenstart showed signs of recovery and one of his first acts was to send, from his sick-bed in the Athole Arms Hotel, a present of some money to the kindly women of Inver who had cared for him and the other passengers. It was warmly appreciated that he should have taken the trouble to show his gratitude so promptly, while still seriously ill. But soon the whole neighbourhood was agog with more exciting gossip about the

Count, a rumour that defied belief and yet seemed to be well-founded. Whether through a remark made by the sick man, or something said by his travelling companions, a whisper spread abroad that Count Roehenstart was none other than the grandson of Prince Charles Edward Stuart, the Young Chevalier for whom the men of Atholl had risen a century before.

Even while the rumour was being hotly debated, fate gave a more tragic turn to events. The Count, who had seemed for several days to be on the mend, collapsed and died on Saturday, 28th October 1854. He was laid to rest in the ruined nave of Dunkeld Cathedral, close to the Wolf of Badenoch, who had disgraced the Stuart dynasty, and Colonel Cleland, who had helped to bring it down. His friends had a gravestone inscribed with his name and title. But the poor women of Inver paid him a more moving tribute; with the money he had sent them, they bought ribbons made from Royal Stuart tartan which they wore for long afterwards, in proud testimony that they had done some small service to the last of the Stuarts at the end of his life.

Were they right to believe so? It seems that they were. The history of Roehenstart's life, though obscure and incomplete, supports the claim that he was indeed Prince Charlie's grandson, even if doubly illegitimate. As may be recalled, the Young Chevalier had a natural daughter by Clementina Walkinshaw, called Charlotte, whom he later created Duchess of Albany — Burns's 'Bonnie Lass of Albanie'. Charlotte, in turn, had an illicit love affair with a dissolute French aristocrat who was also nominally a churchman, Prince Ferdinand de Rohan, Archbishop of Cambrai. By him she had three children: two daughters called Aglae and Zemire, then finally a son, Charles Edward, born around 1784 and named after his illustrious grandfather. The name Roehenstart was a crude combination of Rohan and Stuart.

What happened to Count Roehenstart's sisters is uncertain. He himself led a wandering existence all his life, travelling to many parts of the world, including Russia and America. The obscurity surrounding his origins was due partly to the upheaval caused throughout Europe by the French Revolution, partly by the scandal of his illegitimate birth. Prince Charlie's brother, Cardinal York, did not die until 1807, and the existence of a great-nephew who was the natural son of an archbishop would have been very painful to him. So a certain secrecy surrounded Roehenstart. He was married twice: firstly to an Italian lady, and after her death to an Englishwoman, but

101

apparently had no children. Lady Bute, who knew him, noted his resemblance to Clementina Walkinshaw, his grandmother. Although he probably saw some military service, he was not a general, despite the misleading use of the military title on his tombstone.

So, Charles Edward Stuart, Count Roehenstart, was truly the last of his race. Little more than a century before, his grandfather had marched triumphantly through Dunkeld at the head of a conquering army, on the road, as he thought, to a throne; he passed through again, a few months later, on the way to Culloden. Roehenstart was not destined to take part in such great events and the only public demonstration he ever inspired was the tartan ribbons worn by the women of Inver. Yet that was no mean memorial in its way, and the dust beneath the gravestone in the nave of Dunkeld is the last Stuart that Scotland holds. As the Latin inscription on that plain marble stone proclaims —

Thus passes away earthly glory.

LEGENDS

Gold-Tree and Silver-Tree

There was once a king who had a wife called Silver-tree and a daughter called Gold-tree. One day, Gold-tree and Silver-tree went to a glen where there was a deep pool with a trout in it.

'Troutie, bonnie little fellow,' said Silver-tree, 'am I not the most beautiful queen in the world?'

'Oh, indeed you are not,' replied the fish.

'Who is, then?'

'Gold-tree, your daughter.'

Silver-tree went home, blind with rage. She laid herself upon her bed and swore that she would never be well again until she had eaten the heart and liver of Gold-tree, her daughter. In the evening, the king came home and was told that his wife, Silver-tree, was very ill. He went to her and asked what ailed her.

'Something which you can heal, if you are willing,' she told him.

103

'Indeed,' said her husband earnestly, 'there is nothing I would not do for you, if it is within my power.'

'If I get the heart and liver of Gold-tree, my daughter, to eat, then I shall be well.'

Sorely troubled, the king sent his huntsmen to the hill for a he-goat and gave its heart and liver to his wife, pretending they belonged to Gold-tree. Silver-tree ate the heart and liver, then rose from her bed, restored to health. By good fortune, that same day, the son of a powerful foreign king arrived and asked for Gold-tree's hand in marriage. Her father consented and sent her overseas at once, her mother now believing her to be dead.

A year later, Silver-tree went again to the glen where the pool was with the trout in it.

'Troutie, bonnie little fellow,' said she, 'am I not the most beautiful queen in the world?'

'Oh, indeed you are not,' the trout answered.

'Who is, then?'

'Gold-tree, your daughter.'

'But it is a long time since she was alive. It is a year since I ate her heart and liver.'

'Oh, indeed she is not dead,' the trout told her. 'She is married to a great prince overseas.'

Silver-tree went home and made the king put his longship in order, for she was going to visit her dear Gold-tree whom she had not seen for a long time. The longship was put in trim and they set out. Silver-tree herself was at the helm and she steered so truly that they arrived in no time at all. The prince was out hunting, but Gold-tree recognised her father's longship approaching.

'Oh!' she said to her servants. 'My mother is coming and she will kill me.'

'She will not kill you,' they assured her. 'We will lock you in a room where she will not get near you.'

This was done, then Silver-tree came ashore and began to call out, 'Come and meet your own mother, who has come to see you!'

Gold-tree explained that she could not, as she was locked in the room and could not get out.

'Well,' said Silver-tree, 'will you not put your little finger out through the keyhole, so that your mother may kiss it?'

So Gold-tree put out her little finger, but Silver-tree stabbed it with a poisoned bodkin and her daughter fell dead. When the prince came home and found Gold-tree dead, he was beside himself with grief. She was so beautiful that he would not bury her, but locked her in a room where no one could come near her.

After a time, he married again, when all of his house came under the keeping of his new wife, except for that one room, the key to which he kept himself. One day, however, he forgot to take the key with him and his second wife found her way into the room. And what should she discover there, but the most beautiful woman she had ever set eyes on! She turned her over and noticed the poisoned bodkin in her finger, so she pulled it out and Gold-tree arose, alive and lovely as ever.

At nightfall, the prince came back from hunting, looking very gloomy.

'What will you wager,' his wife asked him, 'that I can make you laugh?'

'Alas,' said the prince sorrowfully, 'nothing could make me laugh, except Gold-tree restored to life.'

'Well, you have her alive, down in that room.'

When the prince saw Gold-tree alive, he was overcome with joy and began to kiss her, over and over again. Then his second wife said, 'Since she is the one you had first, it is better you should remain with her and I shall go away.'

'Indeed, you will not go away,' declared the prince. 'I shall keep both of you.'

At the end of another year, Silver-tree went once more to the glen with the trout-pool and said, 'Troutie, bonnie little fellow, am I not the most beautiful queen in the world?'

'Oh, indeed you are not.'

'Who is, then?'

'Gold-tree, your daughter.'

'But she is no longer alive. It is a year since I stabbed her finger with the poisoned bodkin.'

'Indeed, she is not dead — she is not!' insisted the trout.

So Silver-tree went home and, as before, made the king prepare his longship and herself steered it to the shore where Gold-tree lived. Again, the prince was out hunting, but Gold-tree recognised her father's ship.

'Oh!' she cried. 'My mother is coming and she will kill me.'

'Not at all,' the prince's second wife reassured her. 'We will go down to meet her.'

Silver-tree came ashore, exclaiming, 'Come down, Gold-tree, my love, your mother has brought you a delicious drink!'

'It is the custom in this country,' interposed the second wife, 'that any person offering a drink takes a draught out of it himself first.'

Silver-tree made a feint of putting her lips to it, but the second wife, with a blow, tipped it down her throat, so that she fell dead. All that remained was to carry her body home and bury it. The prince and his two wives lived contentedly and peacefully for a long time after.

The Battle of the Birds

At one time, all the birds and animals came together to fight one another. The son of the King of Tethertown said that he would go to watch the battle and bring back the news of who was to be King of the animals that year. The battle was over, however, by the time he arrived, except for one last fight between a huge black raven and a snake. Since it looked as though the snake would win, the King's son intervened to help the bird by cutting off the serpent's head with a single blow. When the raven got his breath back, he told the King's son, 'For your kindness to me today, I shall show you a spectacle.' Then he ordered the King's son to mount him, and they soared over seven hills, seven glens and seven upland moors.

'Now,' said the raven, 'do you see yonder house? Go to it. A sister of mine lives there and I promise you will be welcome; and if she asks were you at the battle of the birds, say that you were. Then, if she asks if you saw me, say that you did; but make sure that you meet me here, in this place, tomorrow morning.' That night the King's son enjoyed fine hospitality. Next day, the raven took him over another seven hills, seven glens and seven moorlands. They sighted a distant bothy which they reached in no time at all and once again the young man spent the night in great comfort. On the third day, the same thing happened, but next morning, when the King's son went to meet the raven as usual, there was no sign of him. Instead, he found the handsomest youth he had ever seen, carrying a bundle.

The King's son asked him if he had seen a big black raven and the stranger replied, 'You will never see the raven again, for I am he. I

E.Elizabeth MacCallum

Elizabeth Dollen

was under a spell and it was my meeting with you that released me. For that, you will get this bundle. Now you must retrace your steps and spend a night in each house, as you did before; but you must not loose the bundle I am giving you, until you are in the place where you would most want to live.'

So the King's son took the bundle and journeyed back towards his father's house, lodging at night with the raven's sisters, as on his outward journey. When he was drawing near to his father's house and passing through a dense wood, it struck him that the bundle was growing heavier, so he decided to look inside it. To his astonishment, out of the bundle sprang a great castle, surrounded by a lush orchard.

Bitterly now the King's son regretted opening the bundle, for he could not replace the castle inside it, and he would have wanted it to stand in the green hollow opposite his father's house, rather than in this dense wood.

At that same moment, he saw a huge giant striding towards him. 'You have built your house in a bad place, King's son,' said the giant.

'Yes, but I don't want it here,' replied the young man, 'it is only on this spot by accident.'

'What reward would you give me for putting it back in the bundle?' asked the giant.

'What reward would you want?' demanded the King's son.

'Give me the first son born to you when he is seven years old,' said the giant.

'If I have a son,' the youth promised, 'you shall have him.'

Instantly, the giant replaced the castle and orchard inside the bundle. 'Now,' he said, 'go your own road and I shall go mine; but remember your promise, for I shall remember even if you forget.'

So the King's son travelled on until he reached his favourite place and there he emptied the castle and orchard out of his bundle and set it up. When he entered the castle, he found the most beautiful girl he had ever seen.

'Come, King's son,' she said, 'everything is prepared, if you wish to marry me this very night.'

'I am indeed willing,' replied the King's son, and that night they were married.

But after seven years and a day, who should be seen approaching the castle but the giant. The King's son remembered his promise, though until now he had not told his wife about it. She, however, with a woman's resourcefulness, invented a plan to cheat the giant. Instead of giving her own child to the giant, she put his clothes on the cook's son and handed him over. As they walked away from the castle, however, the giant handed the little fellow a rod and asked him, 'If your father had that rod, what would he do with it?'

'He would beat the dogs and cats if they went near the King's food,' replied the boy.

'Why, you are the cook's son!' exclaimed the giant, and he picked him up by the ankles and dashed his brains out on a stone. Then he went back in a rage and swore that, unless they turned over to him the King's son, he would level the castle.

This time they gave him the butler's son. So the giant handed him the rod and asked what his father would do with it. 'He would beat the dogs and cats,' answered the little fellow, 'if they came near the King's bottles and glasses.'

'Ha! You are the butler's son!' roared the giant, and he smashed his skull as well. When he returned to the castle, he was so angry the earth shook beneath his feet. 'Out here with your son!' bawled the giant. So they had, perforce, to surrender the boy, and the giant took him away and brought him up as his own son.

One day, when the lad was fully grown and the giant was away from home, the young man heard music coming from a room at the top of the house. On investigation, he found a beautiful maiden who was a daughter of the giant and who told him to come back at midnight. When he did so, she warned him that the next day he would be offered a choice of her two sisters in marriage, but that he must say that he preferred her, for her father wanted her to marry the son of the King of the Green City, but she did not like him.

Next day, the giant gathered his three daughters and said to the youth, 'Now, son of the King of Tethertown, you have not lost by living with me so long. You will get as a wife one of my two eldest daughters, as well as leave to go home with her the day after the wedding.' But the King's son chose instead the youngest and prettiest. The giant was furious and told him that he must perform three tasks before he could have her.

First, he took him out to the byre, which was foul with the dung of a hundred cattle and had not been cleaned for seven years. He told the King's son that, by nightfall, the byre must be so clean that a golden apple would run from end to end of it, otherwise he would drink his blood instead of giving him his daughter's hand.

The young man started to clean the byre, but it was an impossible task. About noon, when he was blinded with sweat and dropping from exhaustion, the youngest daughter came out to him. She told him to rest at her side and the King's son agreed, since he despaired of completing his task and was resigned to death. He fell asleep and when he awoke the byre was entirely cleaned, so that a golden apple might run from end to end of it.

When the giant returned, he was surprised to find the byre cleaned, but he immediately set the young man his second task: he gave him until the same time the next day to thatch the byre with birds' down, from birds with no two feathers of one colour. From dawn, the King's son was out with his bow and arrow on the moors, hunting birds, but after running about for hours he had only two blackbirds to show for his efforts. Again, the giant's daughter came out to him, he fell asleep and awoke to find the byre fully thatched with feathers.

The giant, needless to say, was far from pleased, but he pressed on and gave the King's son his third task to perform: he was to climb a huge fir-tree beside the loch and bring back, unbroken, the five eggs from a magpie's nest in its top branches. When the youth reached the tree, however, he found it was five hundred feet from its base to the lowest branch. He struggled to climb its trunk, but fell down, bruised and scratched.

Along came the giant's daughter once more, and she thrust her fingers into the tree, forming a ladder which he climbed up to the magpie's nest. The girl was in great fear that her father would find them out and she urged the youth to hurry. As he came back down with the magpie's eggs, she was so nervous that she left her little finger in the top of the tree. But she warned her lover that this could be made useful, for her father would dress her sisters in similar clothes to deceive him, yet he would recognise her by the missing finger.

Since the King's son had accomplished his three tasks, the giant had no choice but to give his permission for their marriage. There was great feasting at the wedding, and then the giant said, 'It is time for you to go to rest, son of the King of Tethertown; take your bride with you from among these.' And he showed him the three sisters who all looked identical, but he knew his wife by the lack of her little finger. As soon as they had retired, however, his bride warned him that they must flee or her father would kill him. So they mounted a blue-grey filly that was in the stable and stole away.

At daylight, they discovered that the giant was pursuing them. The giant's daughter then told her husband to put his hand inside the filly's ear and throw behind him whatever he found there. He found a twig of a sloe-tree which he threw behind him and at once there sprang up twenty miles of thorn-wood.

'My daughter is at her tricks,' grunted the giant, struggling to pass through the dense blackthorn. He had to go home and fetch his big axe and wood-knife, and with these tools he was not long in cutting his way through. 'I will leave the axe and the wood-knife here till I return,' he said, when he had finished.

'If you leave them,' jeered a hoodie-crow in a nearby tree, 'we will steal them.'

Thus, the giant had to go back to his house to store his tools safely, but by noon he was once more gaining on the runaways. Again his daughter told her husband to reach inside the filly's ear and throw what he found behind them. He took out a splinter of stone, which he threw over his shoulder, and immediately there sprang up twenty miles of crags and rock. 'My daughter's tricks are the worst setbacks I ever met,' snarled the giant, turning back home to fetch his crowbar and mighty pickaxe. With these he soon cleared a path, but the hoodie-crow sneered at him again and promised to steal the tools. 'Do so, if you like,' replied the giant, his patience exhausted. 'There is no time to go back.' Seeing her father catching up once more, the giant's daughter told the King's son to reach into the filly's ear for a third time. He did so, and took out a bladder of water which he cast behind him, creating a freshwater loch twenty miles in length and breadth. The giant was running so fast that he could not stop, but plunged straight into the middle of the loch, went under and rose no more.

Next day, the two young people came in sight of the King of Tethertown's house. The giant's daughter urged the King's son to go ahead and tell his family about her. 'But,' she warned, 'let neither man nor beast kiss you, for, if you do, you will forget that you have ever seen me.' So the young man went forward and was reunited with his family and household, and everyone welcomed him warmly. He was careful, too, to warn his parents not to kiss him, but, as ill luck would have it, an old greyhound came in and, recognising him, jumped up at his mouth; after that, he could not remember the giant's daughter.

She, meanwhile, remained seated beside a well where he had left

112

her, but time passed and her husband did not return. At nightfall she climbed into an oak-tree and lay in the fork of it all night. It happened that a shoemaker's house stood close to the well and at noon the next day he asked his wife to fetch him a drink. When the woman bent over the well, she saw the reflection of the girl in the tree above and, mistaking it for her own, thought that she was more beautiful than she had ever realised. So she swaggered back to the house without either vessel or water. 'Where is the water, wife?' asked the shoemaker.

'You shambling, pathetic old clown,' replied his wife scornfully, 'I have been your water and wood-fetching drudge too long!'

The shoemaker, astonished, thought that his wife had gone mad, so he sent his daughter to the well instead. She made the same mistake as her mother and, likewise, returned proud and disobedient. Thinking that his womenfolk had gone soft in the head, the cobbler went himself to the well and saw the reflection of the giant's daughter. Then he understood what had turned the heads of his wife and daughter, but good-naturedly he invited the girl to make herself at home in his bothy, humble as it was.

A few days later, three young gentlemen came to the shoemaker's house to have shoes made, for the King's son had come home and was now to be married. They stared at the sight of the giant's daughter, for they had never seen anyone so lovely. 'That's a pretty daughter you have there,' they said to the cobbler.

'She is pretty, indeed,' he replied, 'but she is no daughter of mine.'

'I would give a hundred pounds to marry her!' cried one of the youths, and both his companions vowed the same. When they had left, the shoemaker told her what they had said and she answered, 'Go after them. I will marry one of them, so let him bring his purse with him.'

So the shoemaker caught up with the three young men and gave them this message. The first youth returned, paid the cobbler a hundred pounds, in dowry as it were, and he and the giant's daughter retired for the night.

As soon as she had lain down, however, she asked the lad to fetch her a drink of water from a tumbler on a shelf at the far end of the bedchamber. He went to do her this service, but found himself transfixed and remained trapped at that end of the room all night, with the vessel of water stuck to his hands. 'Young man,' said the girl, 'why will you not lie down?' But he could not move until

113

daylight. Then the shoemaker came to the door of their room and the giant's daughter asked him to take away this useless boy. That suitor, therefore, slunk off home without telling his companions what had happened.

Next came the second youth and, similarly, when she had lain down, the girl said, 'See if the latch is on the door.' The latch stuck to his hands and he could not move from the door all night; he too went home next morning, shamefaced. The third suitor, who knew nothing of these mishaps, came the next night, and the same thing happened to him: one foot stuck to the floor so that he could not stir all night and next morning he took himself off without a backward glance.

'Now,' said the girl to the shoemaker, 'the sporran of gold is yours; I have no need of it.' The cobbler had the young men's shoes ready and was about to deliver them to the castle, for the King's son was to be married that day. 'I should like to get a sight of the King's son before he marries,' the giant's daughter told the shoemaker.

'Come with me,' he said. 'I know the servants at the castle very well, and you will get a sight of the King's son and all the company.'

Indeed, when the noblemen saw the beautiful woman, they invited her into the wedding-room and gave her a glass of wine. When she made to drink from it, a flame arose from the goblet and two pigeons, one golden and one silver, soared out of it. As they flew round the room, three grains of barley fell to the floor. The silver pigeon ate them up at once. Then the golden pigeon said reproachfully, 'If you recalled how I cleaned out the byre, you would not eat those without giving me a share.' Another three grains of barley fell, and the silver pigeon ate them too. Said the golden pigeon:

'If you remembered how I thatched the byre, you would not eat those without giving me my share.' Three more grains fell, and the silver pigeon gobbled them up as before.

'If you remembered how I harried the magpie's nest,' cried the golden pigeon, 'you would not eat those without giving me my share. I lost my little finger bringing it down and I am missing it still!'

At this recital of his adventures with the giant's daughter, the King's son got his memory back and recognised her at once. Springing to her side, he kissed her hand first, then her lips. So, when the priest came in, they were married for a second time. And there I left them.

The Strong Man's Son

There was once a big fellow whom everyone called the Strong Man of the Wood. He made his living by hunting deer and collecting fuel. One day, an oak-tree that he was cutting down fell over and crushed him, but, with his great strength, he managed to crawl out from under it and stagger to his feet. Then he dragged the tree all the way home, collapsing as he threw it down before his door.

His wife helped him inside and laid him on the bed, but he told her he was mortally injured. He opened his fist, displaying an acorn in the palm of his hand, which he gave to his wife, saying, 'I am going to die, but do you plant this acorn in the dung-heap outside the door. You will have a son, and on the night he is born the sapling from the acorn will rise above ground. You will nourish him on your knee, with the sap from your breast and side, until he becomes so strong that he can tear up the tree grown out of the acorn by its roots.' These were the Strong Man's last words.

When her time came, the widow had a son and she at once asked the midwife whether an oak sapling had appeared out of the ground: it was so. She suckled her son for seven years, then took him out one day and told him to try whether he could uproot the young oak-tree. He struggled to do so, but in vain. So his mother put him to her breast for another seven years, then bade him try again. He tore

DUNCAN MACGILLIVRAY

115

ferociously at the tree, but still its roots held firm. Finally, after another seven years' nourishment, the Strong Man's son made a third attack on the tree. This time he pulled it out by the roots after a few tugs, broke it into firewood and heaped it up beside the door.

Then his mother told him, 'You have sucked the sap of my breast and side long enough; in future you can earn your own living. Come in and I shall bake you a bannock, which you will get with my blessing, and then you must go seek your fortune.'

The youth took the bannock and left home, looking for work as he travelled. Eventually he stopped at a large farm, surrounded by more stacks of corn than he had ever seen, and asked to see the master. When the farmer came, the Big Lad explained that he wanted work. The farmer, who thought him a likely fellow, told him jovially that he could take some of his work off his hands. 'Can you thrash?' he asked. 'Yes,' replied the Lad. So the farmer said he could begin first thing in the morning, but he warned him there was enough corn in the barn to keep two men thrashing for six weeks, besides a yard full of corn-stacks also waiting to be thrashed.

116

After supper, the Big Lad went up to the barn where the men were thrashing and looked at the flails they were using. Then he said to them, 'The flails you have are worthless. When I start tomorrow, wait till you see the flail I shall have.' And he went to the wood and cut himself a flail whose handle was like the mast of a ship.

The hours of work were from the setting to the rising of the stars, but the Big Lad rose before the morning-star had left the sky and began thrashing in the barn so fiercely that he took the roof off. By breakfast-time all the corn in the barn had been thrashed; by dinner-time he had finished the stack-yard too. The farmer was just wondering why his whole steading was blown about with chaff, when the Big Lad came up and told him, to his astonishment, that he had finished all the thrashing. When the farmer went into the barn and saw what had been done, he was afraid; but what frightened him most was the Big Lad's flail.

Next, to his dismay, the Lad told him, 'I must have more food for my dinner than I am getting.' He then demanded a quarter of a chalder (twenty-four bushels) of meal in brose and a quarter of a chalder of meal in bannocks, with a two-year-old ox on alternate days. The frightened farmer agreed, but he and his household knew that they must find some way of getting rid of the Big Lad or his appetite would ruin them.

So he consulted a sage, a very old man of that place called Big Angus of the Rocks. When he heard the farmer's story, he sighed and said that it had long been foretold that they would be ruined by a giant; this must be the prophecy coming true. The means he suggested for destroying the Big Lad was to get him to dig a very deep well and then shovel the earth on top of him while he was still at the bottom of the pit. Next morning, therefore, the farmer set the Strong Man's son to dig a well-shaft. When it was almost finished, the farmer's men crept up and frenziedly shovelled the earth back into the hole, on top of the Big Lad as he stooped at his work. But he stood up in the pit and shouted 'Whish!' whereupon the farmer and his men fled in panic. The Big Lad finished the well-shaft, then returned to the farmhouse, where he was surprised to find his master cowering under the table. To the farmer's relief, he reported that he had completed his work, though he had been disturbed by rooks, as he thought, scratching sand into the hole on top of him.

The farmer went back to Big Angus and described what had happened. 'Then,' said the ancient, 'we will try another plan. Send him to plough the Crooked Ridge of the Field of the Dark Loch. No man or beast ever came back that was ploughing there until sunset.' So the farmer gave this task to the Big Lad, who set out next morning with a plough and two horses for the Field of the Dark Loch. He worked well throughout the day, but towards sunset he heard a loud splashing from the loch and saw a huge, ugly black beast stirring there.

As soon as the sun had gone down, the beast came ashore and made its way along the Crooked Ridge to where the Lad was still unconcernedly ploughing. Despite being warned off by the giant ploughman, the monster lumbered forward and swallowed one of the horses whole. The Big Lad swore that he would make the beast disgorge the horse and an unholy struggle ensued. Though eventually overcome, the beast refused to give up the horse it had swallowed, so the Lad plucked a tree out by its roots and wore it down to splinters belabouring the monster, which still stubbornly retained the horse in its belly. 'Right,' said the Lad, 'I shall make you do the work of the one you have eaten.'

Saying this, he harnessed the beast to the plough and drove it before him until he had ploughed up every last furrow of the Crooked Ridge. Then he led it home to the farmhouse. Meanwhile, the other plough-horse, with its traces broken, had run home before him. Seeing it return alone and frightened, the farmer assumed that the Big Lad was dead.

'The Water-horse of the Dark Loch has made an end of him at last!' he said with satisfaction. Great was his dismay, therefore, when the Strong Man's son arrived back and told him he had ploughed up all of the Crooked Ridge. Worse still, he announced that he had brought the beast back with him and was determined to make it give up the horse it had swallowed. Before the farmer's horrified eyes, he threw the beast on its back, slit open its belly and drew out the horse alive, then hurled the beast into the well-shaft he had dug the previous day and filled in the hole.

The distraught farmer sent for Big Angus of the Rocks and told him what had happened this time. 'We shall give him another try,' said the old man, undeterred. He advised the farmer to tell the Big Lad that the meal had run out and that he would have no food until he himself ground some corn at the mill. He was to use the urgency of the situation as an excuse to make the giant work all night in the Mill of Leckan. 'I'll warrant,' said Angus, 'that the Big Brownie of the Mill of Leckan will not suffer him to return home.'

So the farmer gave the Big Lad these instructions and sent him off with a sled loaded with sacks of corn to be ground at the Mill of Leckan. He reached the mill at dusk and found it shut up, so he roused the miller and told him he had come with a sled of grain which must be ground that night.

'There is not a man on the face of the earth for whom I would open up the mill this night,' replied the miller. Since no amount of urging would change his mind, the Strong Man's son asked him to hand over the key so that he could enter the mill by himself. 'If you enter it,' the miller warned him, 'you will not come out alive.'

'I have no fear at all,' the Big Lad assured him. 'Give me the key.'

The miller gave him the key and he went into the mill. He carried the grain inside, kindled a large peat-fire, put some corn in the kiln, hardened it and put it into the trough. Then he started up the mill, ground as much of the grain as he had dried, sifted it and began to knead some bannocks for himself, since he was hungry. When they were ready, he put them on the kiln to bake.

It was while he was baking them that an ugly-looking creature appeared from a dark corner of the kiln. The Big Lad shouted to him to keep his distance, but, paying no heed, he reached out his paw and

119

snatched one of the bannocks. 'Don't do that again!' cried the Big Lad. But the Brownie paid no attention and a moment later he grabbed another bannock. 'Do that once more,' the Big Lad warned him, 'and I will make you pay dearly for the bannocks.' Indifferent to this threat, the Brownie seized the third bannock. 'Right,' said the Strong Man's son grimly, 'I will make you put back what you have taken!'

With that, he leapt on top of the Brownie and wrestled with him ferociously. As they rolled over and over they upset the kiln and wrecked the mill; people for miles around heard the deafening noise coming from the building. The miller, hearing it in his house, hid beneath the bedclothes, while his wife screamed aloud and crawled under the bed. Finally, the Big Lad overcame the Brownie, who begged him to let him go. 'You will not go free,' the Lad told him, 'until you have repaired the mill and set up the kiln again with the bannocks on it and everything as you first found it.' And to emphasize the point, he gave the Brownie another beating. 'Let me go,' shrieked the Brownie, 'and I shall do everything you tell me!' But the Big Lad insisted on keeping hold of him while he carried out his task.

When the Brownie had put the mill back in order, he said, 'Let me go now, for everything is as I found it.' The Big Lad looked around and asked, 'Where are the bannocks you stole?' Then he beat the Brownie again.

'Let me go,' the Brownie howled, 'you will find the bannocks in the fireplace!' But the Lad still kept a grip on the Brownie while he retrieved the bannocks and put them back on the kiln. After that, he beat him once more for good measure. The Brownie pleaded with him to let him go, promising to leave the mill and never trouble it again.

'Very well,' said the Lad, 'since you have promised that, I shall let you go.' With these words, he shoved him out through the door. The Brownie uttered three ghastly screams and fled. Nearby, the miller heard these screams and his wife cried out from under the bed.

Now the Big Lad ate his bannocks and finished grinding the corn. This done, he loaded the sacks of meal onto his sled and locked up the mill. When he called at the miller's house to return the key, however, the terrified man refused to let him in. So the Big lad simply forced the door and entered the house, saying, 'Here is the key, for I have ground the grain and I am going home.'

The miller peered out fearfully from under the bedclothes and exclaimed, 'How are you alive after being in the mill all night?'

'Pooh!' replied the Strong Man's son. '*You* may go to the mill and stay all night now! I have driven away the creature that was in it and it will never again trouble you or anyone else.'

'Do you hear that, wife?' the miller asked his spouse, but there was no reply. The Big Lad drew her out from under the bed, but she was dead, her heart stopped with terror.

On the way home, the horse drawing the sled faltered, going up the hill overlooking the Mill of Leckan. The Big Lad hit the horse with the back of his hand and accidentally broke the poor beast's shoulder. Struck with remorse, the Lad took the horse out of the traces and placed it on top of the sacks of grain; he then cheerfully drew the overladen sled, by himself, up over the brow of the hill and along the road that led home.

It was this daunting sight that was reported by one of the lookouts whom the farmer who employed the Lad had posted on every road. 'We must leave,' said the farmer in despair, 'for he will kill us all, or at least ruin us.' And so he and all his people fled, leaving the place to the Big Lad.

Soon afterwards, the Strong Man's son came home and unloaded his sled. Surprised to find no sign of life, he searched every nook and cranny of the farm-steading, but found no living soul. He realised then that all had fled and abandoned the place to him.

So the Big Lad thought that he would fetch his mother and bring her back to the fine farmstead which he now possessed. He went, therefore, to the wood where he had been born and told his mother that he had made his fortune and that she must come and stay with him. But she protested that she was old and it was too great a distance for her to walk. 'Not so, mother,' replied her son. 'You carried me for long enough, so I will carry you that far now.' Then he lifted his mother on his back and did not put her down until he reached his new home. There they lived in ease and comfort, and if they are alive they are there still.*

---

*According to one interpretation, there would seem to be a strong element of allegory in this tale. Thus, the Big Lad is the oak-tree personified; his father dies with the old oak, he grows with the sapling. The seven-year intervals in his youth correspond to the periodical thinning-out of an oak wood. Similarly, 'Big Angus of the Rocks' may be an allegorical name for an echo.

Garlatha

Long, long ago, and certainly no later than the eighth century of the Christian era, a goodly prince ruled over the southern part of the 'Long Island' of Lewis, that is to say, Harris. This ruler was widely respected, not only for his bravery, but also because he gave wise judgments, kept the peace and encouraged both hard work and the reciting of poetry.

Equally loved was his wife, a princess called Garlatha, who taught her people skill with crops and herbs, for food and healing, as well as virtue and kindness to the weak. So the land of Harris was a contented country. Unhappily, however, the princess died, leaving an infant daughter who was named after her mother, Garlatha.

As the little princess grew up, it became apparent that she had inherited all her mother's virtues, so that she was as popular in her turn. Time went by, her fame spread and many suitors sought her hand. The ruler of Lewis was hot in pursuit of her, and the chief who reigned in Uist also came in the hope of winning her as his bride.

So one day, her father said to her, 'My daughter, before I die, I want to see you married to a worthy man; I have tried to judge which of the men who have come to see you is the most suitable and I think it will be best if you take the one from Lewis.'

In fact, his daughter preferred the prince from Uist, but the Lewis chief was summoned to marry her. He duly came, well satisfied, the arrangements were completed and the wedding took place. After the ceremony, Garlatha told one of her maids, 'You go in to the celebration and join the company. I am going to hide myself.' Thus, the guests sat down before the feast without the bride, for whom they waited a long time.

Eventually, when they realised that she was not coming, everyone was questioned as to her whereabouts, including the maid, but she could not say where her mistress was to be found. Time was passing, so they searched for her out of doors as well, but without success. Finally, they hunted systematically in every place where she could conceivably be, still in vain. The whole night went by, with the banquet untouched and the guests feeling dismal. Next morning they resumed the search, along the seashore and up in the hills, and continued for days, until there was not a corner where even a bird could sleep, between Barra Head and the Butt of Lewis, that had not been explored; but there was no trace of her.

Garlatha's father wandered about for many years, vainly searching, long after all hope of finding her had vanished. Latterly, he was observed to turn over with his staff every leaf he came across and even to look under ragweed. When he died, she had still not been found.

For about two centuries after this time, Harris was in a state of anarchy. Then MacLeod took possession of it and began to put up new buildings — the old houses had become uninhabitable and roofless. While one of these ruins was being gutted, an old chest was discovered. When it was lifted, the bottom fell away and remained on the ground; it held the skeleton of a woman, with every bone in place, and by its side a wedding-ring as gleaming bright as the day it was put on her finger. The name *Garlatha* engraved on the ring told its own story.

The Master and His Servant

At a period when times were hard, many servants were looking for work, but there was little enough employment to be found. There was a farmer who refused to take on anyone unless he promised to stay in his service for fully seven years and to be contented with no wages, except as much seed corn as he could catch in his mouth while thrashing in the barn. Not surprisingly, nobody would take up this offer.

So at length the farmer grudgingly expanded it by saying that he would also allow the servant to plant the seed he had saved in his best ground and to use his plough and horses for tilling and harrowing the land. At this, a young lad said, 'I'll take your wages.' It was agreed between them, therefore, that the young man was to keep as many grains of seed as he could catch in his mouth while they were beating sheaves in the barn, plant them in the farmer's best land and keep whatever grew from that seed. The next year, he was to add this to the grains he caught in his mouth while thrashing and plant all that he now had in the farmer's best land. It was further agreed that he should have the use of his master's horses, plough and any other gear necessary for planting and reaping his modest crop.

This meagre accumulation was to continue for seven years. In return, the lad was to spend seven winters thrashing in the barn, seven springs sowing, seven summers raising the crop and seven autumns reaping. Whatever was the final harvest from the successive sowings of the youth's seed at the end of seven years, that was to be his wage for all his service.

The young man went home with his employer, but always when he was thrashing in the barn the farmer worked beside him, so that he could only manage to catch three grains of seed in his mouth that first winter. He kept them carefully, however, until the spring, when he planted them in his master's best ground. Out of these grains there grew three ears, and on each ear were threescore good grains of seed.

So the youth put these carefully aside and added to them any grains that he caught in his mouth while thrashing. Next spring, he once more planted all that he had and in the autumn he had as good a crop as the previous year. This too he saved up and again added it to the grains he caught that winter.

And so it went on, year by year, until finally, in the spring of the seventh year, the servant lad planted over every inch of ploughland that his master owned and still had seed left over for sowing. Now the farmer was almost beggared. He had to rent ground from his neighbour so that the youth could plant his surplus seed, and then he was forced to sell off some of his cattle as he had too little land for browsing. Never again, in all his days, did he try to strike that kind of bargain with a servant.*

*Stories about arithmetic progression are common in all folk cultures; here the moral is thrift, as well as the shortsightedness of striking an excessively hard bargain without carefully calculating the eventual outcome. It has been suggested that this tale originally contained a numerical play upon the numbers three, seven and twenty, whose significance has been lost.

What Will Be, Will Be

An astrologer, who travelled widely, arrived one day at a house inhabited by a woman who had a baby girl. When reading the stars that night, he discovered that this little girl was fated one day to become his wife. Since this prospect was displeasing to him, the astrologer resolved to take drastic action to change his destiny. Going back into the house, he offered to buy her baby daughter from the woman for a huge sum of money. Not being a dutiful mother, she immediately accepted his offer and handed over the child. The astrologer then carried off the infant, shut her in a box and threw the box into the sea. Then he departed, satisfied that he had changed the course of fate, as predicted in the stars.

But the box containing the child floated and, before very long, was picked up by a fisherman. He found the little girl inside, took her home to his wife and they adopted her. She grew up extremely beautiful and, at the age of eighteen, entered the service of the local laird.

Now, it happened that the astrologer who had thrown her into the sea many years earlier was an acquaintance of her employer and one night he came to dinner. Intrigued by the exceptional beauty of the girl waiting at table, the astrologer asked his host about her. The laird then related how the fisherman had found her and adopted her. Dismayed, the astrologer recognised her as the child he had tried to kill and realised that he had not yet succeeded in changing his destiny.

Seeking the girl out alone, he led her down to the sea-shore. Then he took a ring from his finger, broke it in two and threw one half into the sea; the other half he placed in his sporran. Turning fiercely to the girl, he warned her, 'If I ever see your face again, without your having the half of the ring which I threw into the sea, I will kill you!' With this menace he left her.

Some time later, the maid went to visit her foster-father in his fisherman's cottage. She was given some fish to dress and cook and, while gutting one, found inside it the half-ring that had been thrown into the sea. Recognising, as the astrologer had less wisely failed to do, the inevitability of fate, she put the fragment of jewellery aside until it would be needed.

Not long after, the astrologer once more visited the laird's house and was enraged to find the maid still in service there. 'Did I not tell you,' he cried, 'that if ever I saw your face again, without having the half-ring, I would kill you?'

'Be calm,' she replied. 'Here is the half-ring for you.' He matched the two halves and discovered that they fitted together perfectly. At last the astrologer realised that it was futile to struggle any longer against his preordained destiny and so he married the girl. And despite the sinister nature of their courtship, they lived together happily ever after, for what will be, will be.

Donald of the Burdens

Donald of the Burdens (*Domhnull nan Cual*) was so named because his work was to gather great loads of fire-wood for the household of a laird. Although he performed this task dutifully, he was sick at heart and secretly very discontented with his lot. One day, as he was staggering homeward, bent beneath a load of wood, he met an elegant young gentleman who saluted him with these words, 'My good Donald, you are exhausting yourself. Are you not getting weary of carrying fire-wood?'

'Yes, indeed!' replied Donald with feeling. 'Very weary. I would not mind a change of occupation.'

'Donald,' the young gentleman told him, 'I am Death. If you take service with me, I will make you a doctor, but on condition that I claim you the first time that you cheat me.' Donald agreed to these terms, for anything seemed better than fetching fire-wood. Then Death gave him these instructions: 'When you go to see a sick man, if you see Death standing at his head, have nothing to do with him, for he will not live; but if Death is standing at his feet, you may take him in hand, for he will recover.'

So Donald did as he had been told and he grew very prosperous. Any patient that he said would live, duly recovered, but any that he declared beyond help invariably died. Then, one day, the King himself became desperately ill. Donald was sent for and arrived at the castle. To his dismay, when he got to the King's bedside, he saw Death standing at his head, so he gave him up for lost. All of the household, however, implored him to do something, so he ordered the King to be turned round in his bed, so that his feet were where his head had been. At once, the King began to improve. Then Donald saw Death creeping down to the other end of the bed, so as to stand once more at the King's head. So he had the King moved round again, and he continued to recover. This game went on for some time, with Donald constantly frustrating every attempt by the dreaded spectre to stand at the King's head. At last, Death departed in a rage.

When the King had completely recovered, Donald left the castle. Before he had gone very far, Death confronted him, saying grimly, 'Now I have you, for you have broken the condition. You have cheated me.'

128

'That is undoubtedly true,' admitted Donald, 'but will you allow me respite until I say my prayers?' Death agreed. 'Then I'll never say them at all!' cried Donald triumphantly. Death was furious at being tricked for a second time, and went off, vowing vengeance.

Donald, however, continued to prosper and suffered no harassment from Death. Daily, his reputation as a medical man was growing greater and he had become a person of great consequence. One day, as he was walking along a quiet road, he met a group of school-children who seemed very downcast. Feeling sorry for them, Donald enquired what was the matter. 'We cannot say our prayer,' they told him, 'and the dominie will punish us.' This was too much for Donald, who immediately sat down by the roadside, gathered the children round him and taught them their prayer.

As soon as the children had departed, Death appeared and said to Donald, 'Now I have you, at all events.'

'You are an amazing fellow,' conceded Donald, 'there's no place where you are absent. They tell me that, even if you were put in a bottle, you would come out and kill.'

'That's true,' Death agreed smugly.

'I don't believe you,' said Donald. 'But I have a bottle here — try whether you can get in.'

Death entered the bottle and Donald rammed the cork tightly in, saying, 'Just you stay in there!' Then he took the bottle and threw it far out into a loch, so that once again he was a free man. But no one can cheat Death indefinitely. Before very long, the bottle was washed ashore, where it was smashed. Death was then let loose once more and he made it his first task to put an end to Donald of the Burdens.

The Enchanted Bridegroom

There was once a wedding and, at the end of the service, the young man who had just been married came out of the church with his bride and the guests, feeling very joyful. At that moment, a tall, dark man, whom he had never seen before, stopped him and asked him to come round to the back of the church, as he wished to speak to him. This was a nuisance, but the bridegroom felt that he could refuse no reasonable request on such a happy day, so he told the rest of the party to go on to the marriage feast and he would soon join them.

When they stood together behind the church, the dark man asked the bridegroom if he would be so good as to stand there until a small piece of candle, which he handed to him, should have burned out. This was undoubtedly a curious demand, but the young man saw at a glance that the tiny stump of candle would burn out in no time at all and that a brief run would enable him to overtake his guests on the road, so he agreed to humour the dark stranger.

As anticipated, the candle took a little less than two minutes, as he judged it, to burn itself out. Then the bridegroom hurried off to find his friends. Coming upon a man cutting turf, he asked him if it was long since the wedding party had passed that way. The man looked puzzled.

'I am not aware,' he said, 'that any wedding party passed here today, nor for a long time past.'

'Oh, there was a marriage today,' the youth assured him, 'and I am the bridegroom. I was asked by a man to go with him to the back of the church, and I went. Now I am running to overtake the party.'

The turf-cutter stared at him with dawning amazement. Then, very quietly, he asked him what date he supposed it was. The bridegroom answered by giving a date that was two hundred years past. It was two centuries, not two minutes, that had gone by while the candle burned.

'I remember,' said the turf-cutter, 'that my grandfather used to relate something of such a disappearance of a bridegroom, a story which his own grandfather had told him as a fact which happened when he was young.'

'*Dhia*! Then I am that bridegroom!' cried the young man, in despair. And with these words, he dissolved where he stood, into a small heap of dust.

A Queer Story

At one time, there was a kiln which stood on the south-west coast of Mull, where men and boys used to get together to play cards, sing songs and tell stories, so that it was really a rude kind of ceilidh-house. The rule there was that everyone who entered the kiln was obliged to tell a story.

One stormy night, as they sat round the fire telling tales, first the owner of the kiln, then each man in the order of seating, a stranger came in who knew nothing of their customs. When it came to his turn to tell a story, he had none to relate, which infuriated the rest of the company. Some of the hot-blooded young men were ready to engage in fisticuffs, but the old man who owned the kiln — more tolerant than his juniors — simply chuckled and told the stranger, who was also a young man, that he could at least make himself useful by going out and stuffing a wad of straw into a hole in the wall that was causing a draught.

Relieved to get out of an ugly situation so easily, the stranger youth gathered up some straw and hurried out to block up the gap in the ancient wall of the kiln, through which the gale was whistling fiercely. As he bent over this task, he happened to glance towards the shore, where he was horrified to see a ship being driven onto the rocks by the storm. He rushed down to the beach and found a small punt into which he clambered and began to row out towards the ship. Before he was half-way to the stricken vessel, however, the

wind suddenly changed direction, so that he was driven off his course and further and further away from land.

Despite his frenzied efforts to row back towards the Mull coastline, he found the wind driving him relentlessly out to sea. All night he drifted and long after that, growing more despairing with each hour. Past Colonsay, Jura and Islay the boat sped, but furiously though he plied the oars as each successive coastline loomed up tantalisingly, he could never succeed in reaching the shore. Eventually, the last of the islands lay astern and he found himself wallowing in the open sea. By now the lad had given himself up for lost, but after a longer space of time than before, yet another coastline appeared on the horizon. Now the unhappy young man rallied his failing strength for one supreme effort with the oars, but, to his great joy, he found that this was hardly necessary, since the wind was carrying him quickly towards land. He could scarcely believe his good fortune when the frail little craft finally grounded in a small creek. Stiff and weary, the young man dragged himself onto dry land, which he knew must be the north coast of Ireland.

About twenty yards inland stood a small cottage to which he made his way, seeking shelter. The occupants of the cottage were an old woman and a girl. They received the young man from Mull very hospitably and explained to him their own sad circumstances. About a month before, the girl's father had died, so that there was no one to work the croft. Now, it did not take any great cleverness to see a mutual interest here: the young man a homeless castaway in a strange land, the old woman and the girl in need of a man to look after them. The solution was obvious, and just a week later the Mull man married the girl and settled down on the croft.

He lived very happily with his wife and — what is perhaps more rare — with his mother-in-law, so that, at the end of four years, they had four fine children. One night, however, he went out fishing, when a gale blew up. To his dismay, he found himself being driven further and further from land, as had happened to him four years before. Then the familiar shapes of the Scottish islands appeared once again — Islay, Jura and Colonsay — but he could not manage to land his boat on their coasts. Finally, to his astonishment, he was driven ashore on Mull at the very point from which he had left; even in the darkness he recognised the place.

The nearest building was the kiln where he had left the storytellers four years earlier and, seeing a light there, he walked up and entered

133

it. He was amazed to find the old man and the whole company sitting inside, in the very places where he had last seen them, with everything looking exactly as it had done before. The old man looked at him quizzically and asked whether he had any story to tell now. So the young fellow replied that, indeed, he had. Then he recounted the tale of his adventures during the last four years and how he had a wife and four children in Ireland.

Since it was not a particularly amusing story, he was taken aback when all the young men in the place burst out laughing at him. But they were silenced when the old man explained to them that the youth had been the victim of an illusion which he had worked on him by means of the black art (*Sgoil dhubh*). So far from being out of the kiln for four years, he had scarce been absent four minutes!

Yet it was a cruel trick that the old man's vanity over his magical powers had caused him to play on the young fellow. For so real had been the impression of the dream that he could never rid himself of the feeling that it had all truly happened. So he went home that night a sad man and ever afterwards he mourned for the wife and children whom, as it seemed to him, he had left in Ireland.

FAIRIES

The Fairies and the Hunchback

There was once a hump-backed man who surprised a band of fairies
dancing in a wood. 'Monday, Tuesday, Wednesday,' they sang in
accompaniment to their dance, 'Monday, Tuesday, Wednesday.'

'Thursday, Friday!' sang out the hunchback, adding to their
refrain. The fairies were delighted with this addition to their rhyme,
which made their dancing even better. So, to show their gratitude,
they removed the hump from the man's back. Straight and tall now,
and handsome too, he strode proudly down his village street, where
he met another hunchback who also lived there.

Astonished by the upright appearance of a man who, only that
morning, had been as deformed as himself, the second hunchback
asked the first how he had got rid of his hump. Then the man who
had been cured explained how the fairies had relieved him of his

135

unsightly burden. Excited by this story, the remaining hunchback determined to befriend the fairies, in the hope that they would make him straight and tall too. Again and again, therefore, he went to the wood and waited there to see the fairies, but always in vain.

At last, however, his patience was rewarded. One twilight evening he came upon them, dancing merrily to the rhyme, 'Monday, Tuesday, Wednesday, Thursday, Friday.'

'Saturday, Sunday!' exclaimed the hunchback. The fairies stopped dancing and looked round to see who had interrupted their revelry. Then, enraged at these new words which spoiled the rhythm of their singing and dancing, they instantly punished the hunchback by adding the first man's discarded hump on top of the second!

Luran Black

Ben Hiant, the Charmed Hill, is a well-known landmark on the south coast of the Ardnamurchan peninsula, just north of the Sound of Mull. At one time, three tenants inhabited the clachans of Sginid and Corryvulin which stood on the shoulder of the hill, and one of them was a man called Luran Black.

One year, Luran began unaccountably to suffer from a strange persecution; every morning, one of his cows was found dead. Now, there was at Corryvulin a grassy hillock known as the Culver, which was widely believed to be inhabited by fairies, so the finger of suspicion pointed at these notorious mischief-makers as the authors of Luran's misfortune. Whatever the case, he could not afford to continue losing a cow every day, so he determined to stay up one night and watch his cattle.

His vigil had not lasted very long before he saw the Culver open and a swarm of little people flood out. They surrounded one of his cows and began to drive it inside their hillock. Luran, curious to investigate the matter further, joined in with them and exerted himself as energetically as two men. The cow was killed and then skinned. Next, an old elf who was squatting in the upper portion of the *dun*, a tailor by trade, with a needle stuck in his right lapel, was seized by his fellows, bundled inside the cow's hide and sewn up; then the indignant, thrashing parcel was rolled down the hillside.

By now the mischievous fairies were in high good humour. They started up a ceilidh and Luran was prominent among the dancers, again conducting himself with the energy of two men. Meanwhile, a number of magnificent cups and dishes were set out on the table. Noticing this, and bearing in mind that the fairies owed him the price of several cows, Luran waited his opportunity, then made off with one of the goblets. Unfortunately, he was seen and the fairies chased after him. One of them sang out:

> Not swift would be Luran
> If it were not the hardness of his bread.

The pursuers had all but caught up with him, when he heard a voice from among them call out some friendly advice:

> Luran, Luran Black,
> Betake thee to the black stones of the shore!

The significance of this, of course, was that no fairy, demon or ghost can venture below high-water mark, so heeding this timely reminder, Luran made for the shore. When he reached the sea, still clutching his stolen goblet, he kept below the fringe of seaweed that was the tide mark and walked home in safety. Behind him, he could hear the yells of the man who had warned him, apparently an old acquaintance who had once been stolen by the elfin folk, being chastised for his interference. Next morning, the missing cow was found lying dead, with its feet in the air, at the foot of the Culver. Remembering the elfin tailor, Luran predicted that a needle would be found in its right shoulder: this turned out to be true, so he forbade any of the beast's flesh to be eaten and threw out the carcase.

But this was not the end of Luran Black's trouble with the fairies. Every year, one of the fields which he tilled in common with his two neighbours was reaped overnight by the little folk as soon as the crop was ripe, so that the benefit of it was lost. So Luran asked an old man who was well-versed in fairy lore to help him. He, therefore, agreed to watch over the crop at night.

As Luran had done, he too saw the knoll of Corryvulin open up and a crowd of people emerge. In command was an old man who allocated work to them in groups: some were set to reap, some to bind, others to make stooks. In this disciplined manner, the field was reaped clean in an amazingly short time. The old sage who was watching this scene on Luran's behalf, however, understood the fairies' ways and how to deal with them. Shouting aloud, he counted the fairy reapers. They vanished immediately and never came near that field again.

Those who make war on the fairies, however, play a dangerous game. Although the feud had not been started by him, Luran had outraged the people of the knoll by penetrating their fortress, stealing one of their splendid goblets, putting a halt to their depredations against his cattle and frustrating their annual harvest of his field. He was a man marked for vengeance and eventually his fate overtook him. Journeying by sea to Inveraray Castle, with his fairy goblet, he was lifted bodily out of the boat and vanished, the cup still in his possession. And that was the last that was ever seen or heard of Luran Black.

The Fairy Snuff-Box

Once upon a time there was a man who lived in Trotternish, in Skye, who discovered that he had run out of snuff. Though he tried all the shops round about, their stock too was exhausted. He was dismayed, for he dearly loved a pinch, but then someone told him that there was a pedlar visiting Kilmuir who had a good stock of snuff. So he went to Kilmuir, only to find that the pedlar had just moved on to Edinbain: when he got there, the pedlar had gone to Dunvegan; when he reached Dunvegan, the pedlar had left for Portree. Finally, he caught up with the travelling man in Portree and bought several pounds of snuff.

On his way home, tired but triumphant, he felt thirsty and went to drink from a stream near the road. Coming back to the highway, he found an old, grey-headed man sitting at the roadside. They passed the time of day and got into conversation, when the snuff-taker described to the old man the inordinate trouble he had undergone to get a few pounds of snuff.

'Well,' said the grey-haired man, 'I will give you a snuff-box, full of snuff, and if you will always give it *open* to others, the snuff in it will never be spent.' With these words, he presented him with a snuff-box. The man from Trotternish thanked the grey-haired stranger and resumed his journey home.

Mindful of what he had been told, he was careful always to offer the snuff-box, open, to other people, and though a long time went by, the amount of snuff in it never diminished. One day, Lord Macdonald came to Trotternish to collect his rent and, while they were transacting their business, as a civility, the man offered his lordship a pinch of snuff. As usual, he was careful to open the box first. Lord Macdonald, however, was irritated by this.

'Would you presume to give the box, open, to me?' he cried. 'Shut it, for I can open it myself.'

Reluctantly, the tenant obeyed and, shutting the box, handed it to the laird. When Lord Macdonald opened it again, he was astonished to find it empty. Then the Trotternish man told the whole story of how he had come by the box and how it had never run out, so long as he opened it before offering it. Ruefully, he explained that it seemed he had now lost a lifetime's free supply of snuff. At this, Lord Macdonald was overcome by remorse that his own high-handedness had inflicted such a loss on his tenant. So, in compensation, he gave him his croft rent-free for the rest of his days, as well as other gifts and benefits.

The Islay Hilt

There was once a sword, the finest blade in all the Highlands — even more renowned than that of Fionn — called the Islay Hilt. This is how it came to be made. Long ago, there lived in Crosprig, near Kilchoman in Islay, a man named MacEachern. He was a smith by trade and had just one son. When this boy came to the age of about fourteen, quite suddenly and inexplicably he took to his bed, where he wasted away, becoming yellow and wrinkled like parchment. No one could understand what ailed him and his father was reduced to despair.

By chance, one day the local wise man (*fear fiosachd*) came into the forge. So the blacksmith confided in him about his son's condition and asked for advice. The wise man pondered about it, then gave his opinion that the wizened boy was not the smith's own son at all, he having been carried off by the fairy folk (*Daoine Sith*) who had left a changeling (*Sibhreach*) in his place.

Nevertheless, before taking any drastic action, it was necessary to make sure that this was really the case. To test things, therefore, the wise man instructed MacEachern as follows: 'Gather as many empty eggshells as you can. Spread them out in front of the creature in the bed and be sure that he sees what you are doing. Then draw water with them, two by two, and arrange them round the fire.'

The blacksmith did all this, in full view of the invalid. At the end of these absurd proceedings, the creature in the bed uttered a shriek of laughter and exclaimed: 'I am eight hundred years old and I have never seen the like of this before!'

Convinced by this evidence that it was indeed a changeling, the wise man then told the smith to kindle a strong fire and throw the creature into the middle of it. If, by any chance, it was his own son, he would cry for help; but if it was a changeling, he would fly up through a hole in the roof. In the event, the wise man's suspicions were proved correct: the fire was lit, the creature was thrown into it and promptly disappeared through the roof.

The problem that remained was to recover MacEachern's true son. It was the wise man's opinion that he must be inside the fairy hill at Borraichill, which would be open only on a certain night (probably Hallowe'en). So, when it came to the appropriate night,

Gwen Dollan

MacEachern the blacksmith set out on his mission, taking with him a Bible, a dirk and a cockerel. As he drew near to the fairy hill, he saw that it was brightly lit up and he heard the sounds of dancing, merriment and wild abandon coming out from the open entrance.

Boldly he walked inside. His Bible protected him from any harm that the fairies might try to do him and he stuck the dirk into the

143

threshold to prevent the entrance from closing behind him. The fairies demanded to know what he wanted, whereupon he replied that he had come for his son and that he would not leave without him, for he had already recognised him among the crowd. At this, the fairies burst into raucous laughter — a great mistake on their part, for it wakened the rooster, who jumped onto the blacksmith's shoulder, flapped his wings and crowed loudly.

Now, the *Daoine Sith* must end all revels at cockcrow, so, in a trice, the fairies disappeared and the hill closed up, but not before MacEachern had seized hold of his son and dragged him outside.

For a year and a day after his return home, the blacksmith's son was listless and scarcely spoke a word to anyone. At the end of that time, however, he was standing in the forge one day, watching his father at the anvil, making a sword, when he suddenly exclaimed: 'That is not the way! Let me do it.' Then, to his father's astonishment, he fashioned the most beautiful sword that was ever seen; the hilt was a masterpiece of craftsmanship, indeed it was perfection. So wonderful a weapon was fit only to belong to the highest in the land and so MacEachern gave it to the Lord of the Isles, whence it became known as the Sword of the Lord of Islay (*Claidheamh Ceann Ile*).

This was enough to make the smith's reputation and all the gentry clamoured for his fine-tempered weapons. His son worked constantly alongside him, employing the skills that he had presumably learned from the fairies to make swords of incomparable quality. Naturally, as befitted their pre-eminence in their craft, the MacEacherns were appointed swordsmiths to the Lords of the Isles and prospered ever afterwards, their fortunes established by the famous Islay Hilt.

WITCHES

Macgillichallum of Raasay

John *Garbh* Macgillichallum of Raasay was an heroic figure. Along with a fine physique, he was endowed with a penetrating mind and great firmness of character. In particular, he was the sworn enemy of all practitioners of the black arts and he had hounded many a witch to her death. Unhappily for Raasay, he had thus become a marked man, the constant object of vengeance, so far as the satanic sisterhood was concerned.

One day, the Laird of Raasay and a group of his friends sailed to Lewis, for the purpose of hunting deer. They enjoyed good sport and spent a merry night on the island, celebrating their fine kill. Next morning at dawn, when they went to the boat, intending to re-embark for Raasay, they found the sea very turbulent. The more cautious members of the party urged a postponement of the journey, but Raasay would not hear of this. Realising, however, that some of his companions needed stiffening of their resolution, he took them to the ferry-house, where they drank several bottles of whisky.

An argument then broke out over whether or not it was foolhardy to venture out to sea in such weather. While the debate was still raging, a wrinkled old woman, bent over a crutch, hobbled into the ferry-house. Raasay appealed to her to give an opinion whether or not the voyage home was a reasonable proposition. She replied firmly that it was, adding some sneering remarks about their faint-heartedness which at once silenced all the doubters and made the party decide unanimously to set sail.

The boat was not far from land, however, before they realised that conditions were much worse than they had imagined. Seeing that they were likely to founder at any moment, they tried to put back to the Lewis shore, but the wind was against them and this proved impossible. On the other hand, it was some slight consolation that the wind was at least carrying them swiftly towards Raasay. Macgillichallum himself took the helm and, encouraging the frightened crew by his own courage and resolution, held the boat firmly on course for Skye, the nearest landfall on their homeward route.

The weather continued to deteriorate, with thunder and lightning added to the rough seas and heavy gale. But the coast of Skye was looming up and Raasay at the helm was steering straight and true, so that the spirits of his passengers began to revive.

Then, to their amazement, a large cat was seen climbing the rigging. A minute later, a second cat appeared and then a third. Those watching now remembered the old woman at the ferry-house and a suspicion of her true nature dawned on them. Soon the shrouds, mast and entire tackle of the boat were covered with cats, to the terror of all on board, who knew that the Laird of Raasay had long been marked for destruction by witches.

Macgillichallum, however, remained undismayed and doggedly held the vessel on course. But even he was filled with horror when a huge black cat, larger than the rest, appeared on the mast-head, in obvious command over the others. Raasay saw at once what was about to happen, so he launched an attack on the army of cats. He was too late. With a combined effort, the cats capsized the boat on her leeward side, so that everyone on board was drowned. Thus, the witches avenged themselves on their inveterate enemy, Macgillichallum of Raasay.

Those of a sceptical disposition might well ask: if there were no survivors, how is it that so much is known of what happened on board Raasay's boat that fatal day? The answer is simple. These details were supplied by the confession of a witch called the Goodwife of Laggan, who participated in the murder of Raasay. Later that same day, while attempting the life of another enemy of witchcraft, in Badenoch, she was mortally injured by her intended victim's dogs. Before dying, she gave an account of her whole satanic career, including the fate of the Laird of Raasay.

'No Evil Comes out of Fire'

There is an old Gaelic proverb which says that 'No evil can come out of fire' (*'Cha tig olc a teine'*) and it was on this principle that the usual method of executing witches was by burning. It was essential that the fire should be pure and unalloyed by any conflicting element. The citizens of Inverness nearly came to grief on one occasion in connection with this rule, when an ill-considered act of charity could have brought the town to destruction.

Inverness, at one time, was particularly plagued by witches, so that the Kirk had frequent recourse to the rigours of the laws against witchcraft. The last witch to be burned at Inverness, in the early years of the eighteenth century, was the notorious *Créibh Mhór*, whose name was long remembered in the town and the countryside round about. But, curiously enough, it was not *Créibh Mhór* herself, but one of her contemporaries, burned shortly before her, who nearly encompassed the ruin of the town.

It happened in this way. After she had been tried and condemned to death in the usual form, the witch was led to the Castle Hill where she was placed on top of a pyre and fastened to a stake. Then the pyre was set alight, since, as the proverb holds, no evil could come out of fire. As the flames crackled upwards and great palls of black smoke began to engulf the witch, she shrieked at the bystanders, for charity's sake, to give her a drink of water to relieve her thirst in the intense heat. A good-natured man in the crowd immediately hurried away, fetched a cup of water and carried it back through the press of people to the execution pyre. As he reached the front rank of the crowd, a man with a reputation for sagacity stopped him and asked what he was doing with the water. When the Good Samaritan explained that he was going to give it to the witch, the wise man seized the cup and emptied it on the ground. Even as the charitable stranger gaped indignantly at this harsh action, he heard the witch give vent to a string of curses, on seeing her stratagem foiled. 'Had I got that mouthful of water,' she lamented, 'I would have turned Inverness into a peat bog!' Then the well-intentioned man understood that, if no evil can come out of fire, it must be a fire that is not

147

even partially quenched and he realised how his thoughtless act had come close to destroying the town of Inverness.

The Evil Lady of Ardvreck

At some time in the eighteenth century, the dilapidated Ardvreck Castle, in Assynt, was occupied by an elderly dowager who had an evil reputation and who caused endless trouble and dissension in the neighbourhood. There was a married couple who lived not far from the castle, but for several years they were fortunate enough to escape the old lady's attention and things went well enough for them. This changed, however, when a child was born to them. The Lady of Ardvreck spread a rumour that the wife had been unfaithful to her husband and that the child was not his. The man, instead of recognising this as a malicious lie, allowed his mind to become poisoned by suspicion, reproached his wife with infidelity and even threatened to kill the baby.

Greatly distressed, his wife wrote to two of her brothers who lived a considerable distance away, and they both arrived on a visit a few days later. They protested their sister's innocence, but her husband stubbornly refused to be convinced.

At last, the younger brother, a much-travelled man who had lived for years in Italy, said, 'We have but one resource. Let us pass this evening in the manner we have passed so many happy ones before, and visit tomorrow the old Lady of Ardvreck.' He promised that he would confront her with someone as clever as herself and they should discover the truth.

Next day, they set out for the castle, a grey, whinstone pile

149

standing partly on a promontory and partly rising out of a narrow loch, situated between two hills. The old lady treated them with pretended graciousness and answered their questions about their sister with seeming frankness. Guests and hostess were seated in the low, arched hall of the castle, its narrow, unglazed windows over-looking the loch. It was a bright, sunny day, with a cloudless sky. Finally, seeing the wicked old lady immovable in her calumny, the younger brother said to her, 'You can have no objection that we put the matter to the proof, by calling in a mutual acquaintance?'

Since the old woman assented, the younger brother got up, bent towards the stone flags on the floor and began writing on them with his finger, murmuring all the while in an unknown language. As he did so, the loch outside became turbulent and a mist rose up from it which blotted out the sky. Then a tall, black figure appeared, standing against the wall.

The brother turned to the husband. 'Now,' he told him, 'put your questions to *that*, but make haste.' Though the husband was sorely afraid, his curiosity about his wife was so consuming that he managed to croak out the question whether she had remained faithful to him. The apparition answered that she had.

No sooner had the mysterious figure spoken, than a terrible storm broke upon the castle; a huge wave from the loch burst through the windows, hail beat upon the roof and turrets, and the flagstones of the hall heaved beneath their feet. 'He will not leave us without his *bountith*,' the brother explained to the old lady. 'Whom can you best spare?'

The Lady of Ardvreck, with faltering steps, opened the door of the hall and, at that moment, a little orphan girl who worked in the castle came running in, alarmed by the storm. The Lady pointed at her.

'No, not the orphan!' cried the apparition. 'I dare not take her.' At that, another giant wave from the loch swept through the hall, half swamping it with water.

'Then take the old witch herself!' yelled the elder brother desper-ately, pointing at Lady Ardvreck. 'Take her!'

'She is already mine,' the spectre replied implacably, 'but her time is scarce up yet. I take with me, however, one whom your sister will miss more.'

With these words, the unearthly visitor vanished and the tempest subsided. What puzzled the frightened people in the castle hall,

though, was that none of their number was missing. Surely the dread stranger had not departed without his *bountith*? When they returned home, however, they discovered the melancholy outcome: the baby, the question of whose paternity had been the cause of all the trouble, had died at the same moment when the dark spirit had disappeared from the hall of Ardvreck Castle.

According to tradition, for five years after these events all the grain that grew in Assynt was black and withered, and no herrings were to be found in the lochs. When the five years had passed, Ardvreck Castle was destroyed by a mysterious fire and the Evil Lady died in the conflagration. Thereafter, nature resumed its course; the corn grew golden and the waters of Assynt teemed with herrings once more.

Mór Bhàn

There once lived in Assynt two witches who were among the foremost practitioners of the black arts. By chance, they had both become witches at the same time and for the same reason. In their youth, they were two of the bonniest girls in that part of the country, but they fell in love with the same young man. One day, while they were working together in the fields, the man that they both loved went past on the road. 'Yon is my lad,' remarked one of the girls.

'No,' objected the other, 'he is *my* lad!'

Thereupon they fell to quarrelling, and eventually to striking and scratching each other. Finally they tugged out handfuls of hair from each other's scalps, and one, as she threw a hank of her opponent's hair to the four winds, shouted aloud to be given powers of witchcraft. Not to be outdone, the other girl made the same demand, and from that moment both girls became witches.

It was generally acknowledged, however, that the one called *Mór Bhàn* (Fair Sarah) was the more powerful. Her neighbours noticed that she had fresh fish whenever she wanted it, also milk, butter and cheese when no one else had any. Since it was well known that witches could divert milk from their neighbours' cows to themselves, or get it out of the couplings supporting the rooftree of the house, people drew their own conclusions.

But *Mór Bhàn* also had power over the wind. Once, when some fishermen from Farr were in Assynt, they could not return because of contrary winds. So one of them took *Mór Bhàn* a present and asked her to use her powers to create favourable winds. She went to their boat and ordered them to hoist sail; then she took the sheet rope and tied three knots in it. That done, she told them to put to sea and, when they were out from the shore, to untie one of the knots if they wanted a favourable wind. If they then desired an even better wind, they should untie the second knot; but on no account must they untie the third knot until they were ashore in their home port.

The fishermen set sail and, following her instructions, untied two of the knots in succession, with the result that they made good speed homeward. When they were within fifty yards of the shore, however, one of the crew, overcome by curiosity about the third knot, secretly untied it. Instantly he disappeared. When the boat came to shore, his shipmates searched everywhere for him, but in vain, although they had all seen him only a few minutes before. Baffled by this mystery, they finally abandoned their search and went to their homes. Next day, the missing man's body was found some fifty yards from the shore; clearly he had paid the penalty for disobeying Fair Sarah.

Mór Bhàn herself also suffered a punishment for her witchcraft. As has been said, one of the benefits of her evil powers was that she could get the best of food when others went without. One morning, she served fresh herrings for breakfast to her son, an upstanding young man who had no truck with the black arts. He was puzzled to see the fish, for the weather had been so stormy of late that no boats had been able to put to sea. When he asked his mother where they had come from, she replied brusquely, 'Never you mind where I got them — just you eat them!'

Obediently, then, the young man sat down at the table. Before starting breakfast, however, he closed his eyes and said grace. When he opened his eyes, he was revolted to see that, in place of the fine herrings, his plate held horse-dung! His mother's evil powers had transformed the dung into herrings, but the prayer he had said had broken the spell and revealed its true nature.

Horrified, the youth realised that his mother was a witch, and he left home for ever that same morning; later, it is said, he served as a soldier in the Peninsular War. In this way, *Mór Bhàn*, who had enjoyed so many benefits as a consequence of her pact with the Devil, lost what was dearest to her, ironically, by the exercise of that same power.

The Black Cats of Gilean

In the district of Waternish, in the north of Skye, there is a tiny place called Gilean. It happened once, many generations ago, that there was a wedding celebration there, attended by all the local people. The only person left out was a small boy of about twelve years of age, who stayed at home to herd cattle.

That evening, when his work was done, the boy came back alone to his parents' cottage and ate a hasty supper. Then he damped down the fire and climbed into the box-bed which he occupied in a corner of the room. There was a pot of porridge hanging over the fire and three bowls of milk on the dresser. Happily, the boy snuggled down in bed, anticipating a good night's sleep.

He was still lying awake, however, at about midnight, when a surprising thing happened. Three black cats jumped in through the window and crept over to the dresser; jumping up onto it, they started to drink the creamy milk. Then, while the boy watched, the three cats suddenly turned into women. What was even more astonishing, he recognised all three of them as women from Gilean!

At that moment, they realised that the boy was awake and watching them. So they crossed the room and stood over his bed. Fiercely they warned him that if he told anyone what he had seen he would meet with a horrible death. The terrified boy promised that he would never breathe a word of it to a living soul and the three strange visitors left.

A year passed and the boy told no one about his frightening experience. But he could not rid himself of the memory of it and it preyed on his mind so that he could not sleep at nights. As time passed, so far from feeling easier, he fretted about it more and more. At last, unable to bear the burden of his secret alone any longer, he went to his mother and told her what had happened, despite the dreadful warning he had had to keep silent. This sharing of his knowledge made him feel better.

Shortly afterwards, the boy had to go to a cattle sale in Portree. That night, to the alarm of his family, he did not return. Next morning, when men went out to search for him, he was found lying dead, his body horribly mutilated. What most puzzled those who

found him was that his wounds appeared to be made by the claws of cats.

The people of Gilean built a cairn to his memory at the place where his body was found. It can still be seen today — *Carn na Gilean*, the Cairn of Gilean.

THE DEVIL
AND THE SUPERNATURAL

Macphie of Colonsay

Macphie of Colonsay was out hunting one day and was overtaken by darkness before he could get home. Seeing a light, he made towards it and found a group of men sitting around a grey-haired old one. 'Macphie, come forward!' the old man called out. Macphie obeyed and caught sight of a beautiful bitch, the finest he had ever seen, with a litter of pups. One jet-black pup in particular was splendid beyond comparison.

'This dog will be mine,' said Macphie, coveting the pup.

'No,' the old man told him, 'you will get your choice of the pups, except for that one.'

'I will not take any but this,' Macphie insisted.

Then the old man said: 'Since you are determined to have it, it will only serve you for one day, but it will do that service well.'

He told Macphie to return on a certain night and he would give him the pup. So Macphie went back on the appointed date and the old man handed over the jet-black pup, saying, 'Take care of it well, for it will only serve you the one day.'

As the months passed, the Black Dog turned into the largest and most beautiful beast ever seen. But every day that Macphie went out hunting, he would call the Black Dog, which would come as far as the door, then turn back and lie down again, for it was only destined to serve its master on a single day. Macphie's friends were forever telling him to kill the Black Dog, for it did not earn its food, but he always refused, saying that the Black Dog's day would yet come.

One day, a band of gentlemen arrived from Islay and invited Macphie to join them in a hunting expedition to Jura, which at that time was uninhabited and a rich hunting-ground for deer. There were sixteen of these spirited young huntsmen and Macphie gladly joined them. When he called the Black Dog, however, it refused as usual to go beyond the door. Each of his companions called it in turn, but it would not budge. 'Shoot it!' cried the young gentlemen impatiently, but Macphie refused, still keeping his faith in the Black Dog's future service. When they reached the shore, they found that a wind had risen so that they could not cross to Jura that day.

On the morrow, as they set out, they called the Black Dog as before, but with the same result. 'Kill it,' urged the hunters, 'and don't be feeding it any longer!' But Macphie still demurred. Again the weather prevented them from sailing to Jura.

'The Dog has foresight,' said the hunters sarcastically.

'It foresees that its day will yet come,' replied Macphie.

On the third day, the storm had passed away and the weather was fine. Without troubling to call the dog this time, they made their way to the shore and launched the boat. To their surprise, the Black Dog came bounding down the beach with a ferocious expression and leapt into the boat. 'The Black Dog's day is approaching,' observed Macphie thoughtfully.

They spent the night on Jura, camping in a cavern known as the Big Cave. The following day was spent hunting deer, with the success that was usual on that island. In the evening, they dined off venison around a fire in the Big Cave, there being a large hole in the roof which conveniently served as a chimney. After supper, the young men lay down, while Macphie stood warming the back of his legs at the fire. Then each of the youths began to say that he wished his beloved was there that night. 'Well,' said Macphie contentedly, 'I prefer that my wife should be in her own house. It is enough for me to be here myself tonight.'

No sooner had he said these words, than he was astonished to see sixteen women entering the cave. The torches went out and only the uncertain flicker ôf the fire illuminated the cavern. The strange women went over to where Macphie's companions lay, but he could distinguish nothing in the darkness and no sound came from the other men. Then the women rose and came back into the firelight; one of them stood in front of Macphie, as though making ready to attack him.

At this, the Black Dog sprang up with a terrifying expression and, snarling ferociously, launched itself at her. All the women then fled from the cave, pursued by the dog. When the last of them had vanished, the Black Dog returned from the mouth of the cave and settled at Macphie's feet. Macphie himself, still in semi-darkness and shocked by these uncanny happenings, had scarcely had time to gather his wits when he was terrified by a ghastly noise above his head. It sounded as though the roof of the cavern was about to fall in. Looking up, he saw a horrible hand coming down through the hole in the roof, as if to snatch him up and lift him bodily out of the cave.

Once again, however, the Black Dog intervened. Leaping up, it sank its teeth into the grisly arm, between elbow and shoulder, and a desperate struggle ensued. Eventually, in its ferocity, the Black Dog gnawed clean through the arm so that the dreadful Hand fell to the cavern floor. Then, with an even more frightful noise than before, the creature that was above the cave lumbered away, Macphie thinking again that the roof was bound to collapse. The Black Dog ran out of the cave in pursuit of its prey, leaving Macphie alone. He was full of apprehension and wished that the dog had stayed to guard him, but he had no more frightening visitors that night.

At dawn, the Black Dog came back to the cave, lay down at Macphie's feet and expired within a few minutes. By the light of the new day Macphie was now able to look around the cave, when he found to his grief that all sixteen of his companions lay dead. So, taking the grisly Hand with him as evidence of what had happened, Macphie went down to his boat and sailed alone back to Colonsay. When the folk there saw the Hand, they marvelled that such a hideous thing could exist. It was then their sad duty to send a boat back to Jura and bring home the bodies from the Big Cave.

Macphie, however, was at least vindicated in his steadfast refusal to kill the Black Dog, without whose protection he did not doubt that he too would have lain dead on Jura. This must surely be the origin of the Gaelic proverb *'Thig latha a choinduibh fhathast'*, 'The Black Dog's day will come yet'.

To Sup with the Devil

In ancient times, one of the most sinister methods of conjuring up the Devil was the barbarous ritual known as the *taghairm*. Its purpose was to force the Nameless One to appear and either grant a wish to the individuals who had had the audacity to perform the rite, or to answer a question which they put to him. The ceremony consisted of roasting a number of cats alive on a spit and was known as 'giving his supper to the Devil'.

According to tradition, the *taghairm* was once performed in a large barn at Pennygown, in the isle of Mull, by two men — Lachlan *Odhar* and his companion Allan, son of Hector. As they roasted several cats on spits, the tormented creatures set up a terrible screaming; presently other cats came into the barn and joined in the howling, until the noise was so dreadful that Lachlan and his companion were nearly unnerved by it. Then the biggest of the cats began to speak, saying, 'When my brother, the Devil, comes — '

'Away, cat!' shouted Allan, son of Hector, before the animal could say any more. Then, in an expression that was to become a Highland proverb for concentrating on the immediate task, he called to Lachlan, 'Whatever you see or hear, keep the cat turning!' (*Ge b'e dè a chì no chluinneas tu, cùm an cat mu'n cuairt!*)

'I will still wait for him — and his son too!' replied Lachlan, regaining his courage.

Finally, the Devil stood among the other cats on the rafters of the barn and, while they kept a respectful silence, declared, 'Lachlan *Odhar*, son of Donald, son of Neil, that is bad treatment of a cat.'

But Lachlan's comrade, Allan, cried again, 'Whatever you see or hear, keep the cat turning!' So they went on with the grisly proceedings until the Devil, seeing that they were in danger of succeeding, sprang to the floor with fearful menaces. Lachlan, however, intrepidly struck the cat on the head with the hilt of his claymore, exclaiming, 'The cross of the sword in your head, wretch!' Defeated, the Devil appeared in his proper shape and asked the two resolute conjurors what they would have from him. Allan asked, 'Prosperity and children'.

Lachlan demanded, 'Prosperity upon prosperity, and a long life to enjoy it.'

Compelled to grant their requests, the Devil ran out of the door, shouting exasperatedly, 'Prosperity! Prosperity! Prosperity!'

And so it turned out; both men had their wishes granted, but to be sure of holding the Devil to his bargain they repeated the *taghairm* every year. On one occasion a couple from the island of Coll, knowing of Lachlan's prosperity and his influence with the Devil, came to beg a yoke of horses from him. Lachlan denied this request, but when the two suitors left, he sent one of his henchmen to eavesdrop on their conversation. 'What a wild eye that man had,' he overheard the woman say. Her husband answered, 'Did you suppose it would be an eye of tenderness, rather than a soldier's eye, as is fitting?' When this was repeated to Lachlan, he summoned the couple back and gave them their yoke of horses.

When Lachlan *Odhar* was dying, his nephew was anxious to make him repent his pact with the Devil and renounce his Satanic connection. So he walked through a stream near his uncle's house and went in to see him, with water still running out of his shoes.

His nephew then pretended that he had met Allan, son of Hector, who had helped Lachlan perform the *taghairm* and who by now had been dead for some time, along with the ghost of another man connected with the diabolic ceremony, not far from the house. He had been forced to cross the running stream several times in order to escape from them, he explained. As they pursued him, they had warned him that they were now in the bad place and that they were waiting for his uncle, who would soon have to join them, unless he repented.

To this, the old man contemptuously replied, 'If I and my two companions were there and we had three short swords that would neither bend nor break, there is not a devil in the place that we would not take prisoner.' These defiant words finally convinced his nephew that Lachlan *Odhar* would never repent having gained his earthly goods by giving his supper to the Devil.

The Brahan Seer

Of all the possessors of the gift of 'second sight' (*Taibhsearachd*), the most celebrated of all time was *Coinneach Odhar Fiosaiche*, or Kenneth Mackenzie, whose fame has gone down to posterity under the title of the Brahan Seer.

Kenneth Mackenzie was born in the early seventeenth century and worked as a farm servant on the Brahan estate, near Loch Ussie, in Ross-shire, a territory ruled by the Mackenzies of Seaforth. He had an unusually sharp tongue for one of his lowly station and this earned him the hatred of his shrewish mistress, the farmer's wife. Eventually, she decided to dispose of him with poison. One day, he was sent out to cut peats in a place far from the farmhouse, so that his dinner had to be carried out to him by his wife. Unknown to her, their mistress had poisoned the meal, which consisted of sowens and milk.

For some reason, Mackenzie's wife was late in setting out, so that it was well past her husband's usual dinner hour. He, made well aware of the fact by the rumbling of his belly, left off his labours and sat down on a hummock. Within minutes, he had fallen asleep.

From this slumber he awoke suddenly, feeling something very cold against his breast. Opening his clothes, he discovered a small white stone, with a hole through the centre. Peering into it, he saw a vision which warned him of the poisoning of his food by the farmer's wife.

162

D. MACLEOD

From that moment, he had the gift of second sight, but he had to pay a forfeit for this privilege: the eye with which he had first looked through the stone was blinded. His other eye, however, showed him that his wife had come while he slept and left his dinner for him to find when he should waken. To test the truth of the vision he had seen, he gave the food to his collie dog, which died in agony shortly afterwards.

Kenneth, made restless by his unlooked-for gift, now embarked on a nomadic life, wandering the countryside and uttering prophecies, generally of a baleful nature. Others were simply a foretelling of certain developments that would take place in his native countryside. He is said, for example, to have predicted the building of the Caledonian Canal in the words: 'The day will come when English mares, with hempen bridles, shall be led round the back of Tomnahurich.' Similarly, he forecast the railway through the Muir of Ord in this verse:

> When there shall be two churches in the parish of Ferrintosh,
> And a hand with two thumbs in *I-Stiana*,
> Two bridges at Conon of the gormandisers,
> And a man with two navels at Dunean,
> Soldiers will come from Tarradale
> On a chariot without horse or bridle,
> Which will leave the Muir of Ord a wilderness,
> Spilling blood with many knives;
> And the raven shall drink his three fulls
> Of the blood of the Gael from the Stone of *Fionn*.

Now, the blood-bath in the last part of the stanza never seems to have materialised, but the remainder of the prophecy does appear to have been fulfilled. Two churches were built at Ferrintosh and, according to eye-witnesses in the nineteenth century, a man with two navels was living at *I-Stiana*, in the Black Isle, and a man with two thumbs on each hand not far from Dunean. The 'chariot' has been widely interpreted as the railway trains and Kenneth was also reported as having said 'That he would not like to live when a black, bridle-less horse would pass through the Muir of Ord.' An ominous prediction which was tragically fulfilled was his claim 'that the day will come when the Big Sheep will overrun the country until they strike the northern sea.' Whether this refers to sheep or deer is uncertain, but it is true in either case.

More particularly, *Coinneach Odhar* foretold that Tomnahurich, the mustering-place of the Frasers and reputed to be a fairy hill, 'would be under lock and key, and the fairies secured within'. This, on the face of it, must have seemed a very unlikely eventuality in the seventeenth century; later, however, it became enclosed as a cemetery to serve the town of Inverness. At Petty, there was a huge stone weighing more than eight tons, which at one time marked the boundary between the estates of Culloden and Moray. Mackenzie prophesied:

> that the day will come when the Stone of Petty, large though it is, and high and dry upon the land as it appears to people today, will be suddenly found as far advanced into the sea as it now lies away from it inland, and no one will see it removed, or be able to account for its sudden and marvellous transportation.

On the night of 20th February 1799, the Stone of Petty was mysteriously displaced and carried about two hundred and sixty yards out to sea. No one could agree whether it was caused by an earthquake, by the action of ice, by a terrible gale which blew up that night or by diabolic intervention; but the Brahan Seer had predicted the incident.

It is only fair to add that many of the Brahan Seer's prophecies have remained blatantly unfulfilled and with the passing of the social conditions to which some of them specifically appertain — for example, clan warfare — it is now impossible that they should ever be realised. On the other hand, others did give the appearance of being strikingly borne out. Of the Mackenzies of Rosehaugh, Kenneth *Odhar* prophesied:

> The heir of the Mackenzies will take
> A white rook out of the wood,
> And will take a wife from a music-house
> With his people against him!
> And the heir will be great
> In deeds and as an orator,
> When the Pope in Rome
> Will be cast off his throne.

This prediction is typical of the mixture of foresight and nonsense which characterised so much of the Seer's claims. A later Mackenzie of Rosehaugh married a girl from a music saloon and was much resented for doing so; Sir George Mackenzie of Rosehaugh, who lived in the lifetime of the Brahan Seer, became Lord Advocate of

Scotland in the reign of Charles II; but the Pope could only be said to have been deposed from his temporal throne in the nineteenth century — successively by Napoleon Bonaparte, the 1848 Revolution and the Risorgimento in 1870 — none of which was contemporary with the great lawyer.

There was one outstanding prophecy of the Brahan Seer, however, whose poignant accuracy could not be disputed by any Scot. Walking one day across Culloden Moor, he cried out:

> Oh! Drummossie, thy bleak moor will, ere many generations pass away, be stained with the best blood of the Highlands. Glad am I that I will not see that day, for it will be a fearful time; heads will be cut off by the score, and no mercy will be shown or quarter given on either side.

A prediction which caused Kenneth to be ridiculed in his own lifetime, by reason of its patent absurdity, concerned the Mackenzies of Fairburn. Addressing a large number of people one day, the Seer declared:

> Strange as it may appear to all those who hear me this day, yet what I am about to tell you is true and will come to pass at the appointed time. The day will come when a cow will give birth to a calf in the topmost chamber of Fairburn Castle. The child now unborn will see it.

At this time, the Mackenzies of Fairburn were rich and powerful, and the Seer's prophecy that they would lose their estates and become all but extinct seemed far-fetched. Prosperity in the turbulent Highlands was of so precarious a tenure, however, that most open-minded people would have admitted the possibility that this family's fortunes might collapse; what provoked total incredulity was the claim that a cow would calve at the top of Fairburn Tower. Despite the abuse heaped on him, though, Mackenzie refused to retract this statement.

More than a century passed and, although the Mackenzies no longer lived in Fairburn Tower, the most sensational part of the prophecy remained unfulfilled. The tower became derelict and its doors fell in, but the stone staircase was still more or less intact. One day, the tenant farmer who lived nearby carried straw up to the top of the tower for storage. It was an untidy business and by the time he had finished the whole stairway was littered with straw. A few days later, one of his cows strayed in through the broken door and began to pick up the straw, slowly following the trail upstairs. Eventually, having reached the uppermost chamber, she was unable to get down again, being heavily in calf. So she had to be left there until her calf was born, after which mother and offspring were both brought down safely, having precisely fulfilled the prophecy of *Coinneach Odhar*.

Ironically, Kenneth's gift of second sight brought about his own terrible end, the victim of an act of barbarity exceptional even by the standards of seventeenth-century Scotland. His own clan chief, Kenneth, 3rd Earl of Seaforth, was a staunch royalist who led an unsuccessful rebellion against Cromwell in 1654. For this he was imprisoned until the Restoration. Shortly after being set at liberty, he had occasion to go to France on business, leaving his estates and his seat, Brahan Castle, under the supervision of his wife Isabella, also a Mackenzie and sister to the first Earl of Cromartie. She was a proud, jealous and cruel woman, as *Coinneach Odhar* was to learn to his cost.

While Lord Seaforth dallied in Paris, enjoying the varied amusements of that elegant city, his wife grew daily more impatient. This impatience was aggravated by the fact that her husband neglected even to write to her, although he had been away for several months longer than originally intended. In a desperate attempt to discover where Lord Seaforth might be, and how employed, the Countess sent to Strathpeffer, summoning *Coinneach Odhar* to Brahan Castle, in the hope that his powers of divination could throw some light on the matter.

Arrived at the castle, Kenneth was brought before Lady Seaforth, who demanded that he furnish her with news of her absent husband. He asked where Lord Seaforth was supposed to be and declared that he thought he could find him, provided he was still alive. Then he put the magic stone (*Clach fhiosrachd*) to his eye and laughed aloud at what he saw. 'Fear not for your lord,' he told the Countess, 'he is safe and sound, well and hearty, merry and happy.'

Pleased to hear that her husband was safe, Lady Seaforth then pressed the Seer to describe his surroundings and what he was doing.

'Be satisfied,' said Kenneth. 'Ask no questions; let it suffice you to know that your lord is well and merry.'

'But where is he? Who is with him? Is he preparing to come home?' she persisted.

166

'Your lord is in a splendid room,' the Seer told her, 'in very fine company and far too pleasantly employed at the moment to think of leaving Paris.'

Kenneth had always had a sharp tongue and misanthropic disposition. On this occasion, there was an ironic tone to his voice which disturbed Lady Seaforth. Convinced that he was concealing some unpleasantness, she bullied and cajoled him until at last the Seer said:

> As you insist on knowing that which will make you unhappy, I must tell you the truth. My lord seems to have little thought of you, or of his children, or of his Highland home. I saw him in a gaily gilded room, finely dressed in velvet, silk, and cloth of gold, and on his knees before a fair lady, his arm round her waist, and her hand pressed to his lips.

This disclosure of her husband's infidelity made Lady Seaforth mad with rage. Besides being jealous, she was mortified that these words had been uttered in front of her servants, who would soon make her shame known throughout the Highlands. She determined at all costs to discredit Mackenzie by giving the strongest imaginable testimony of her faith in her husband — whom she believed in her heart to be guilty — by exacting extreme retribution from the Seer, as his supposed calumniator. Shrieking at him that he had vilified the nobility, slandered a great chief among his clansmen, abused her hospitality and sullied her husband's name at his very ancestral hearth, she concluded, 'You shall suffer the most signal vengeance I can inflict — you shall suffer death!'

Mackenzie could scarcely believe his ears. At first, he was inclined to think that this was an hysterical outburst on the part of the Countess, which would subside within a few hours. He was deceived. Preparations for his execution went ahead forthwith; Lady Seaforth was within her rights of feudal jurisdiction. Tradition is at variance as to the means of execution employed. One version holds that *Coinneach Odhar* was simply hanged; another, more enduring, tradition asserts that the witchcraft laws were invoked against him and that he was led to Chanonry Point, where he was burned to death in a tar-barrel. Perhaps mention should be made of yet another account, which claims that his sentence of death was the consequence, not of revealing Lord Seaforth's unfaithfulness, but of disparaging a group of children, Lady Seaforth's and others, who were pointed out to

167

him as examples of aristocratic beauty and breeding. To this, the Seer is reported to have replied sourly that 'he saw more in the company of the children of footmen and grooms than of the children of gentlemen'. While such a remark would have been typical of the misanthropic Seer and might well have brought him to the unfavourable notice of Lady Seaforth, it is unlikely that even the arbitrary feudal justice of the seventeenth century would have found grounds in it for a capital sentence.

In any case, *Coinneach Odhar* soon came to the realisation that the Countess was in earnest and that his death was imminent. On the scaffold, he took the magical white stone and put it to his single eye for the last time. Then he uttered his final, dark prophecy, presaging the downfall of his enemies:

> I see into the far future, and I read the doom of the race of my oppressor. The long-descended line of Seaforth will, ere many generations have passed, end in extinction and in sorrow. I see a Chief, the last of his house, both deaf and dumb. He will be the father of three fair sons, all of whom he will follow to the tomb. He will live care-worn and die mourning, knowing that the honours of his line are to be extinguished for ever, and that no future Chief of the Mackenzies shall bear rule at Brahan or in Kintail. After lamenting over the last and most promising of his sons, he himself shall sink into the grave, and the remnant of his possessions shall be inherited by a white-hooded lassie from the East; and she is to kill her sister. And as a sign by which it may be known that these things are coming to pass, there shall be four great lairds in the days of the last deaf and dumb Seaforth — Gairloch, Chisholm, Grant and Raasay — of whom one shall be buck-toothed, another hare-lipped, another half-witted, and the fourth a stammerer. Chiefs distinguished by these personal marks shall be the allies and neighbours of the last Seaforth; and when he looks round him and sees them, he may know that his sons are doomed to death, that his broad lands shall pass away to the stranger, and that his race shall come to an end.

When the Brahan Seer had finished speaking, he threw the white stone into a small loch beside the place of execution, declaring that whoever should find it would similarly be gifted with second sight. Then he submitted stoically to his fate. It was long held in the

168

neighbourhood that the precise site of Kenneth Mackenzie's death was a large stone slab, which became covered in sand, a few yards east of the road from Fortrose to Fort George Ferry, about two hundred and fifty yards north-west of the old lighthouse.

What, then, happened to the Mackenzies of Seaforth? Was the Seer's dire prophecy fulfilled? The last Earl of Seaforth was born in 1754. While at school, he suffered an attack of scarlet fever which left him deaf for the rest of his life; latterly, he was also dumb. It is said that, of four lairds who were his contemporaries, Sir Hector Mackenzie of Gairloch was buck-toothed, The Chisholm of the day was hare-lipped, Grant was half-witted and Raasay a stammerer. Lord Seaforth had three sons, all of whom predeceased him. When he himself died, on 11th January 1815, his earldom became extinct and the Seaforth estates were inherited by a cousin, who had married Admiral Sir Samuel *Hood*. She was widowed at about the same time that Lord Seaforth died, so that she returned from India, in widow's weeds, to take up her inheritance. Was this the 'white-hooded lassie from the East'? Finally, years later, Mrs Stewart Mackenzie (as she had become by re-marriage) was driving her younger sister, Caroline, in a pony carriage, near Brahan Castle, when the horses bolted. Both women were thrown out of the carriage and the younger later died of her injuries. Thus, the heiress could, in a sense, be held responsible for the death of her sister.

Even allowing for certain niceties of interpretation which are perhaps necessary to mould some of these incidents to the precise pattern of Mackenzie's predictions, the fact remains that the whole course of events, within a single generation, conformed strikingly to the prophecy.

Coincidence, of course, is a strange thing, but it has never found favour as an explanation of uncanny happenings in the Highlands. To the local people, the significance of it all was perfectly clear: the dying prophecy of the Brahan Seer had at last encompassed the downfall of the House of Seaforth.

The Lady of Balconie

The estate of Balconie, in the seventeenth century, was owned by a laird who had married a woman of very mysterious character. Few people ever got to know her and those who did were united in regarding her as a most disquieting person. Preferring solitary walks to human society, she spent much of her time wandering along the banks of the River Auldgrande, which followed a tortuous course through a deep gorge a few miles from Balconie, on its way to the Cromarty Firth.

After the lapse of some years, however, the Lady of Balconie suddenly seemed to discover a need for companionship and she made a favourite of one of her maids, who became a kind of confidante. The girl, a simple Highland lass, was by no means pleased by the position in which she found herself. Although a maid might normally think herself fortunate in being favoured by her mistress, Lady Balconie was so gloomy and forbidding a creature that the girl was really afraid of her and dreaded the hours spent alone in her company, which their new intimacy imposed. She felt, as she expressed it, that she was in the presence of a being who belonged to another world.

Late one afternoon, after a day spent in melancholy silence, Lady Balconie quit the house and, ordering her maid to accompany her, set out for the banks of the Auldgrande. They reached the deep gorge exactly at sunset, when the lady spoke for the first time since leaving home. 'Let us approach nearer the edge,' she said. The frightened maid protested that the sun was setting and that strange things had reportedly been seen in the chasm after nightfall. 'Pshaw!' exclaimed her mistress. 'How can you believe such stories? Come, I will show you a path that leads down to the water. It is one of the finest places in the world. I have seen it a thousand times and must see it again tonight.'

With these words, she seized hold of her shrieking maid and, with more than ordinary strength, began to drag her towards the edge of the gorge. As the two women struggled, a man's voice suddenly spoke to Lady Balconie, saying, 'Suffer me, ma'am, to accompany you. Your surety, you may remember, must be a willing one.' The swooning maid looked round and saw a saturnine man, dressed in green, standing beside them. Then, to her further astonishment, her mistress released her grasp on her and, instead, with a look of despair, allowed the stranger to lead her towards the edge of the precipice. At the brink, she turned round and detached from her belt the ring of household keys, which she threw up the bank towards her maid; the bunch of keys struck against a large granite boulder and left their own impression upon the stone, as if it had been wax. Then the Lady of Balconie cast a final glance at the setting sun and disappeared with the green-clad stranger into the chasm.

When the maid tottered home and told the amazing story of what she had witnessed, the Laird of Balconie rushed to the gorge with all the men of his household. They searched by torchlight all night and continued the search for several days. At the edge of the precipice they found an almost uprooted bush and there was a line scratched in the moss of the cliff-face a few yards below. Above all, there was the startling evidence of the imprint of the keys in the large boulder. But of Lady Balconie there was no trace. Eventually, baffled and grieving, the searchers gave up.

Ten years passed, without any light being shed on the mystery. Then, one day, a middle-aged man called Donald, who was servant to a maiden lady who lived nearby, was fishing in the Auldgrande, a little downstream from the gorge. Donald was not particularly well paid, for his mistress was a miserly old woman, so he felt justified in helping himself to a few fish for his elderly mother. So, as his luck was good that day, he selected the best fish and hid them under a bush, taking the remainder home to his stingy mistress. She asked him sharply whether these were all he had caught and he assured her that he had brought home all his catch. Since it was actually a very respectable quantity of fish, the old spinster grudgingly accepted his word.

As soon as he could get away, Donald hurried back to his hiding-place to recover his cache of fish. When he looked under the bush, however, he found to his astonishment that the fish had gone. A slight trail across the grass, glinting here and there with fish-scales, betrayed that an animal had dragged them off in the direction of the gorge. Determined to track down the marauder who had deprived his mother of her supper, Donald followed the trail down the shallow banks of the river until he found a path he had never noticed before, leading upstream towards the chasm. As he walked along the water's edge, the banks rose precipitously on either side; at times, he

MURRAY WILSON

could scarcely see the sky, as foliage high up on the overhanging crags obscured it. By now, the gorge had grown so narrow and gloomy that Donald could no longer clearly distinguish the path. He was on the point of turning back, when, upon rounding an outcrop of rock, he found himself in the entrance to an enormous cave.

As he entered the cavern, blinking with amazement, two huge dogs rose on either side of the cave-mouth, stared at him, then lay down again without harming him. Inside, he found a rusted iron table and chair. But it was not these commonplace furnishings which made Donald's eyes dilate in astonishment, but the objects which they supported: on the table lay his fish and a large mound of dough, ready for baking; in the chair was seated the Lady of Balconie.

'Donald!' she cried, recognising him immediately. 'What brings you here?' Donald explained that he was looking for his fish, but wondered, in turn, what could detain her ladyship there. 'Come away with me,' he urged, 'and I will take you home, and you will be Lady of Balconie again.'

'No, no!' she told him. 'That day is past — I am fixed to this seat and all the Highlands could not raise me from it.'

Donald examined the iron chair. It was embedded in the rock; underneath it lay a rusty chain, one end attached to a ring in the cavern floor, the other end around one of Lady Balconie's ankles. She warned Donald that not only had his fish fallen forfeit to her gaoler, but he would be hard put to it to escape himself. 'Look at those dogs!' she exclaimed. In fact, the two great hounds had risen again from the floor and, in contrast to their former indifference, were now watching him warily. 'I maun first durk the twa tykes, I'm thinking,' Donald observed phlegmatically.

The lady told him that that was not the way and warned him to be ready. Then she snatched up the heap of dough from the table, tore it in two and threw a piece to each of the dogs, signalling urgently to Donald to run from the cave. When he reached the path outside, he turned for an instant to bid the unhappy lady farewell before scrambling away up the river-bank.

Soon he found himself following a narrower, more precipitous and treacherous route than he remembered taking on his way to the cave. He realised then that he had strayed from the original path and he was never again able to discover it. Dusk was deepening into night when he finally struggled, breathless and dishevelled, onto level ground above the gorge. But he knew that he could not find the cavern if he ever attempted to go back, for the secret path was lost to him. So there the Lady of Balconie has remained a prisoner to this day.

The Black Officer of Ballychroan

People are inclined to attach a mystical importance to any kind of watershed in time: the seasonal solstices, the turn of a century or, even more significant, the end of a millenium. So it was not to be wondered at that many strange rumours attached themselves to a tragedy which took place at Gaick, in Badenoch, during the night of 31st December 1800. Although, on the face of it, a natural catastrophe, the coincidence of the date (which many reckoned as being the last day of the eighteenth century) and the reputation of the principal character involved, all combined to create an atmosphere of mystery and doom.

Captain Macpherson of Ballychroan, popularly known as the 'Black Officer of Ballychroan', was widely feared. He was an army officer who had abandoned his wife and children and who was reputed to have torture-chambers beneath his house, from which the screams of his victims could be heard at night by passers-by. One account describes him simply as a 'dark savage'.

Towards the end of the year 1800, and not long before the catastrophe which overtook him at the turn of the century, Captain Macpherson went on a hunting expedition with some friends to the Gaick hills in Badenoch. The countryside was wild and uninhabited, there being no dwelling-house for thirty miles around. The only shelter available to the hunters was a mean hut, maintained for this purpose, where men whose enthusiasm for shooting game outstripped their fondness for comfort could pass the night.

This particular hunting party, however, spent the night not only in discomfort, but almost in terror. About midnight, the occupants heard strange noises all around the flimsy lodge and it sounded as if the roof was likely to be smashed in. At first there was a weird slashing sound, then another noise, graphically described by one witness as resembling a fishing-rod beating violently on the roof. All the dogs in the hut were overcome by terror and their masters were more than a little unnerved.

The Black Officer, however, went boldly outside, where one of his servants overheard him speaking to some unknown being who answered in the voice of a he-goat. The Devil, as the quaking servant assumed it to be, rebuked Macpherson for not bringing more men with him; to this, the Black Officer replied that he would come again with more people. After that, he returned to the hut and the mysterious noises subsided.

When the Black Officer organised another shooting party shortly afterwards, he had some difficulty in persuading others to accompany him. The servant who had overheard his conversation refused utterly to join this expedition and he was echoed by all but one of the men who had been in the lodge at Gaick that terrifying night. The sole exception was a man called Macfarlane, an exemplary Christian and altogether of a very different stamp from the Black Officer. Possibly his own clear conscience led him to dismiss fears of diabolic intervention. Other men who had not been present on the previous occasion accepted Captain Macpherson's invitation and so, at the very end of the year, the Black Officer set out once more for Gaick, accompanied by a respectable number of gentlemen and servants. It was noted that on this day Captain Macpherson left his keys and watch at home, which he had never done in his whole life before; it was as if he knew that he would have no further use for them.

No one knows for certain what happened that night of 31st December 1800, at the hunting-lodge at Gaick, for none survived to tell. So far as any natural cause could be ascribed to the disaster, it appears that some kind of whirlwind, of phenomenal force, struck the hut and scattered it in fragments over an unbelievably wide area. Some idea of the strength of the hurricane may be conveyed by the fact that the bodies of the occupants were found scattered at distances of half a mile from the site of the lodge. Even the barrels of the hunters' guns were mangled and the bodies were only discovered by the accident of an occasional hand or limb protruding from the snowdrifts. Macfarlane's body was carried a greater distance than any of the others and was not found until a day later. To find his corpse, the searchers employed a man who once before had discovered a dead man in the hills, for it was generally believed that someone who had found a body already would be more likely to find one again.

When the bodies were being carried home, the elements kept up an eerie harassment and a continual rainstorm swept around the melancholy cortege, so strongly that it was eventually forced to halt. Captain Macpherson's body was being carried at the head of the procession; when the order was changed and the Black Officer's corpse was borne further back, the storm abated sufficiently for the bearers to proceed.

Such was the mysterious and grisly end of the ill-reputed Captain Macpherson. His epitaph was succinctly expressed in one of the songs composed about the tragedy:

> The Black Officer of Ballychroan it was,
> He turned his back on wife and children;
> Had he fallen in the wars in France,
>   The loss was not so lamentable.

Black Ian, Son of Donald of the Songs

Ian *Dubh* MacLeod, brother of Neil MacLeod, the celebrated Skye poet, and himself no mean versifier, was born in Glendale. Black Ian — described by some as black in looks and black in nature — practised mesmerism or hypnosis. It was his own sinister boast that grass would never grow on his grave. (In fact, he was buried in America and grass *did* grow over his remains.)

Black Ian was a sailor and it was generally believed that he had learned his mesmeric arts from some Chinese shipmates. He must have been as ill-regarded at sea as on land, for during one of his voyages the rest of the crew tried to throw him overboard, but he eluded capture and commemorated the episode in a song he later wrote:

> They tried to drown me —
> They had no success.

Another time, Ian was on leave in Glasgow when he gave an amusing demonstration of his skill as a conjuror. He and a friend went into a fruit shop, where Ian bought an orange. Then he produced a knife, cut the orange in half and took out a sixpence from the centre. Feigning delight at this, he bought two more oranges and, before the astonished gaze of the shopkeeper, extracted sixpence from each of them as well. After that, they left the shop, but came back about an hour later and peered through the window: to their glee, they saw the shopkeeper sitting disconsolately among the débris of his entire stock of oranges, every one of which he had chopped up in a futile quest for sixpences!

Some of Black Ian's tricks, however, were downright uncanny and seemed to justify his nickname — 'The Wizard of the North'. On another visit to Glasgow, for example, he met a friend in the street, who invited him to come for a drink, but also warned him that he had only sixpence in his pocket. Ian, in fact, had no money at all, but he told his friend to hand over the sixpence and everything would be arranged satisfactorily. Such was the authority of Black Ian that his friend complied and followed him into a public-house. There, the sixpence appeared to be mysteriously transformed into a sovereign, so that generous quantities of drink flowed all evening until both Ian and his companion were totally incapacitated. No one could ever explain how Ian had worked this extraordinary illusion,

but it is said that he later went back and reimbursed the publican for his loss.

There was always a sinister atmosphere surrounding Black Ian and people were terrified of him. Behind his back, they whispered stories of his strange powers of hypnosis, conjuring and telepathy. On one occasion, it was rumoured, his sisters were boiling a chicken in a pot over an open fire, when the chicken, startlingly, began to crow. 'Ah,' said one of the sisters, 'Ian is coming home.' Shortly afterwards, he walked in the door. Such were the happenings that made a legend of Ian *Dubh*, son of Donald of the Songs, whose weird gifts and adventurous life are still talked about with awe in Skye and the other islands to this day.

178

GHOSTS

The Skull of Saddell

Saddell, in Kintyre, was long regarded in times past as a place of religious importance. The church at Saddell, from as far back as anyone could remember, held a grisly relic — a human skull, kept permanently on display as a *memento mori*, a constant reminder that death finally claims all men and that there is no escape.

At one time, a farmer who lived two or three miles away at Barr was enraged to discover that his son had fallen in love with the servant-girl who worked in their house. Determined to prevent this unsuitable match, he racked his brains for months, trying to think of a plan to turn his son against the girl.

One winter night, a great blizzard swept across Kintyre, so that all the folk huddled in their houses, glad to be safely indoors. As the farmer sat round the fire with his household, an idea came to him at last for discrediting the maid-servant in his son's eyes. Knowing that no man, let alone a frail girl, would dare venture out into the storm, especially on so terrifying a mission as he was about to propose, the farmer offered his maid this grim bargain: 'If, before the day breaks, you bring me the skull that is in Saddell Church, you shall have my son for your husband.'

To her master's astonishment, the girl rose at once, wrapped her plaid around her and left the house. So ferocious was the blizzard that she could scarcely make any headway against the howling gale, but she remembered that she must return with the skull before dawn and so, bent nearly double, she struggled on through the snowstorm.

At last, frozen and exhausted, she arrived at the church. Here she was assailed by new terrors. The churchyard was a fearful place on that pitch-black night, with the snowflakes whirling round it like souls in flight and the wind wailing among the tombs. But most frightening of all was the church itself. The door stood mysteriously open, as though beckoning the girl to enter, while inside the ancient kirk she could hear a rustling sound, as of many unseen creatures waiting for her. The maid hesitated on the threshold with fast-beating heart and her courage nearly failed.

179

Then she thought of the farmer's son and, steeling herself, she stumbled into the blind darkness of the church. All around her now she could hear movements. What were these beings that surrounded her? Were they devils? Had the dead risen from their graves in the churchyard, wakened by the fury of the storm? As she felt her way down the aisle, her arms held out blindly before her, she was almost sure that these invisible watchers brushed against her several times, so that she had to bite back a scream. Only the thought that she was in a holy place where God must watch over her, and the determination to win the man she loved gave her the strength to go on.

Finally she groped her way to the skull and, hooking her frozen fingers into its empty eye-sockets, she snatched it up and wrapped it inside her plaid. Then, clutching this prize against her breast, she

S. MACDONALD.

staggered back to the door of the church. The mysterious creatures seemed to be thicker around her than before — she could even feel their warm breath on her cheek. Yet they did her no harm and made way for her until she finally found herself out in the churchyard once more.

After the darkness inside the church, even the blizzard-swept countryside appeared less terrifying. The return journey too, as is always the case, seemed shorter and the hard pressure of the skull inside her plaid was a constant reminder to the girl that she had accomplished her task, if only she could get back to the farm before dawn. Hope lent wings to her feet and in a surprisingly short time she sighted the welcoming lights of the farmhouse. Anxiously she glanced up at the sky: it was as dark as when she had set out. By bringing the skull home before dawn, she had passed the test that her master had set her.

Almost dead from cold and exhaustion, the maid-servant beat feebly on the door and, when it was opened, fell forward into the cheering warmth and light. Before she would even let the rest of the household carry her to the fire and chafe her frozen limbs, however, the girl took the skull from inside her plaid and showed it to the farmer. He was dumbfounded at the sight. It seemed incredible to him that anyone — especially a chit of a girl — could have had the courage and resolution to make such a nightmare journey and take the gruesome relic from a deserted church at dead of night. So, fearing some trick, he immediately sent a party of men to discover whether the skull was truly removed from Saddell.

When they reached the church, they found that the gale had blown open the door and a herd of deer was sheltering inside. It was these innocent beasts that the girl had sensed all around her when she took the skull, which the searchers confirmed was missing from its place.

All doubts removed, the farmer now realised how deeply the servant-girl must love his son and he gave his consent to their marriage, which very soon took place. In this way, from being a grim reminder of death, the skull of Saddell was changed into a memorial of true love.

A False Suitor

On St. Mungo's Island, at the entrance to Loch Leven, near Glencoe, there is a burial ground beside a ruined church, said to have been built as a penitential exercise by one of the Camerons of Lochiel. During the eighteenth century, it was the site of a bizarre supernatural event.

A man who had just been buried there kept the whole neighbourhood awake for several nights after his funeral, calling on a certain person, by name, to come and help him. Eventually, the man who had been summoned decided to do as he was bidden, so he made his way at dead of night to the new grave. When he got there, he was astonished to find the head and neck of the dead man protruding above the ground.

'What is your business with me,' he asked the corpse, 'and why are you disturbing the neighbourhood with your untimely lamentations in this fashion?'

The dead man replied, 'I have not had rest, night or day, since I lay here — nor shall I, so long as this head is on my body. I shall tell you why. In my younger days, I swore most solemnly that I would marry a certain woman and that I never would forsake her, so long as this head remained on my body. At the time, I had hold of a button and, the moment we parted, I severed the head of the button from the neck, thinking that all was then well. I now discover my mistake. You must, therefore, cut off my head.'

Taking pity on the dead man's predicament, his friend braced himself, then cut off the head of the corpse, close against the ground, with one stroke. At this, relieved of his burden, the forsworn suitor lowered the trunk of his body back down into the grave, abandoning his severed head.

Ewen of the Little Head

The Macleans, who live on the island of Mull, are said to be descended from two brothers who lived in the fourteenth century. Lachlan *Lùbanach* (the Crafty) founded the chiefly line of Duart, in the eastern part of the island, while Hector *Reaganach* (the Stubborn) was progenitor of the Maclaines of Lochbuie, on the south coast. The Lochbuie Maclaines (they have used this distinctive spelling since the sixteenth century) have always claimed that their ancestor Hector *Reaganach* was the elder brother and that they are in fact the senior line, although the Macleans of Duart have always held the chiefship. This may be the reason why, in the early days, there was much feuding and ill-will between the two branches.

Even if he could not become chief of his name, Hector *Reaganach* was determined to win for himself and his descendants a great territory on Mull. So he obtained a grant of Lochbuie from the Lord of the Isles. At that time, however, Lochbuie was held by the MacFadyens, who had no intention of surrendering their inheritance tamely to an interloper. Hector, for his part, decided to use guile rather than force. He approached MacFadyen humbly and asked for just enough ground to build a sheep-fold. Glad to be able to buy off Maclaine with so modest a concession, MacFadyen readily gave him a hillock. On this mound Hector *Reaganach* built, not a sheep-fold, but a castle, from which he harassed the MacFadyens. One day he even shot an arrow from its walls which narrowly missed Mac-Fadyen as he sat nearby, picking meat from the bones at his dinner. Eventually, worn down by Hector's continued attacks, MacFadyen had to abandon his lands of Lochbuie and retire to Garmony, north of Duart, where he found a new occupation minting gold coins. His descendants became known as the Seed of the Goldsmith.

No sooner were the Maclaines firmly settled in Lochbuie and quit of their feud with the MacFadyens, than they quarrelled with their cousins the Macleans of Duart. The main cause was a tract of land which lay between the territories of the two families and to which both laid claim. One day, when a man from Lochbuie was ploughing the disputed land, a friend of Lachlan *Lùbanach* of Duart shot him dead with an arrow. This crime was made the more serious by the fact that the murdered man was related to the wife of Hector

Reaganach. She had not long to wait for her revenge. Shortly afterwards, Lachlan *Lùbanach*'s two sons visited Lochbuie. When the time came for them to leave, Hector's wife insisted on walking part of the way home with them. Presently they reached a well, where she cut off the heads of the two children and dropped them down the well-shaft, leaving the headless corpses on the ground. Ever afterwards, this place was known as 'The Well of Heads' (*Tobar nan Ceann*).

After this outrage the feud between the two houses became bitter and deadly. But the trouble was aggravated by the behaviour of Hector *Reaganach*'s son Ewen and his unpopular wife. Ewen was brave in battle, but rather stupid. His head was too small for his body (clearly betraying the limited size of his brain), from which he gained the nickname Ewen of the Little Head (*Eòghann a' Chinn Bhig*). The clansmen used to chuckle at this and quote the old saying, 'A big head on a wise man and a hen's head on a fool'. Like many fools, however, Ewen often came out with remarks which contained a twisted kind of wit. For example, at his mother's funeral he told the pall-bearers not to carry the body so high, 'in case she should seek to make a habit of it'. This gave rise to the proverb 'to seek to make a habit of anything, like Ewen Little Head's mother'.

The most foolish action of Ewen's life, however, was his marriage to a sour and ambitious woman, of the house of Macdougall of Lorn. The nicknames she earned are a guide to her character — 'Stingy, the Bad Black Heron', 'The Black-bottomed Heron', 'The Macdougall Heron', and so on. As if her personality did not make her a sufficiently unsuitable bride for the heir of Lochbuie, the Black Heron suffered from another disqualification; she was foster-sister to Maclean of Duart's wife, so that, in the clan feud, her sympathies were not with her husband's kin.

By now, between the murderous behaviour of his wife, the stupidity of his son and the ill-nature of his daughter-in-law, Hector *Reaganach* of Lochbuie was finding family life intolerable. So, on the pretext of granting Ewen some independence, he gave him the lands of Morinish as his patrimony. Consequently, Ewen left his father's stronghold of Moy Castle at Lochbuie and built himself a castle on an islet in a small loch called Sguabain, between Lochbuie and Duart. Here, as master of his own small estate, the slow-witted Ewen was contented enough, but not so his shrewish wife. The Macdougall Heron, as has been said, felt no loyalty to the house of Lochbuie, but she was faithful to her own interests. If her husband were somehow cheated of his inheritance, she would become a woman of no account.

Brooding on this, day after day, she became obsessed with the fear that Ewen would lose the succession to Lochbuie and that, when his father died, it would be seized by the Macleans of Duart and united to their lands. So she nagged at Ewen, giving him no peace, until at last he agreed to go to his father and demand from him the title deeds to Lochbuie. Hector *Reaganach* promised him patiently that he would inherit all of Lochbuie and Ewen returned home reassured. His wife, however, was not at all satisfied and she insisted that he was letting himself be gulled by false promises and that his uncle, Lachlan *Lùbanach* of Duart, would assuredly usurp his inheritance. Goaded by this harpie, Ewen went to see his father again and they had a violent quarrel, which reached a climax when he struck his aged parent a stunning blow on the head.

It was, of course, a scandalous thing for Ewen to have struck the venerable chief, who was also his own father, in a fit of rage. When Lachlan of Duart heard about it, he saw his opportunity not only to put down that troublesome young cub who was his nephew, but also to join the lands of Lochbuie to his already large estates. He determined, therefore, to march against Ewen, intending either to kill or imprison him and then assume the chiefship of all the Maclean lands on Mull. In this way, the very thing that the Black Heron had dreaded was brought about by her nagging interference.

Fighting, at any rate, was the one art in which the dull Ewen excelled, so he mustered his men and made ready to do battle. On the evening before the opposing forces were to meet, Ewen went walking by himself. Presently he came to a stream, where he saw a fairy woman washing clothes and crooning the 'Song of the Macleans'. Her elfin nature was betrayed by the incredibly pendulous breasts which hung down before her — the people of Mull have long known that the fairy womenfolk of the island can be recognised by this freak of nature — so that from time to time she flung them over her shoulders as they impeded her laundering. Ewen knew the correct way to placate the fairy and, creeping up behind her, he grasped one breast and placed the teat in his mouth, crying, 'Yourself and I be witness you are my first nursing mother!'

'The hand of your father and grandfather be upon you,' answered the fairy. 'You had need that it is so.'

185

'What are you doing?' wondered Ewen, and was chilled by her reply.

'Washing the clothes of those who will mount the horses tomorrow and will not return.'

Ewen asked anxiously, 'Will I win the fight?'

To this, and to his other questions, the elf woman gave the mysterious kind of answers these folk delight in. She told him that if he and his men were served butter at their breakfast, without asking for it, he would win; if not, he would lose. When he asked whether he would survive the battle, she evaded the question. Before she left him, however, the fairy bestowed on him a parting gift, as she called it. This was nothing less than the destiny, in every generation, to give warning of approaching death to all his race.

Disturbed by this encounter, Ewen went home in a thoughtful frame of mind. Next morning, resolved to make the best possible showing that day, he put on a new suit of clothes. No sooner had he done so than a serving-woman came in, admired his new clothing and said, 'May you enjoy and wear it.'

Now, although this compliment was well-meant, it was traditionally unlucky for a woman to be the first to say this. So Ewen, already unnerved by his meeting with the fairy, snapped at her, 'May you not enjoy your health!'

At breakfast, remembering the fairy's prediction, Ewen watched anxiously to see whether butter was served, though he knew that he must not ask for it or he would doom himself to lose the battle. Unhappily, even on this important day when her husband and the menfolk of his household were to be put to a severe trial, 'Stingy, the Bad Black Heron' lived up to her ungracious reputation. She served a breakfast of curds and milk, without even troubling to supply spoons, telling the men to put on hens' bills to peck up their food. Ewen lingered, hoping against hope that someone would think of sending in butter, but none came. Finally he lost his temper and threw his shoe on the floor, shouting in exasperation, 'Neither shoes nor speech will move a bad housekeeper!' He then sealed his own fate by calling for the butter, adding bitterly, 'You may eat it yourself tomorrow.'

His wife replied contemptuously, 'He who kicks old shoes will not leave skin upon palm.'

Then the butter was brought, but Ewen declared that he did not want her curds or cheese seeping in white clots through his men's sides, kicked open the door of the dairy and let in the dogs. After this outburst, he and his men went off, without having touched the breakfast. It may readily be imagined that seldom has a warrior gone into battle with a heavier foreboding of defeat than Ewen Maclaine that morning.

And so it happened that Ewen of the Little Head, the dullard whose only talent was for fighting, failed even on the battlefield. He and his men met the Duart Macleans at *Onoc nan Sgolb*, near Torness, in Glen More. Ewen was dispirited by the belief that he was fated to lose the battle and his men were the weaker for not having break-fasted. When the fight was joined, a slashing stroke from a broad-sword cut off the upper part of Ewen's head, so that he who had impiously given his father and chief a buffet on the temple was himself decapitated.

But Ewen did not fall dead on the ground. Instead, he leaped upon his horse, a small black beast with a white spot on its forehead, and galloped off the field. From that day, he fulfilled the grim destiny imposed on him by the fairy woman, bringing warning of death to the Maclaines of Lochbuie. Whenever one of the sept lay dying, Ewen of the Little Head could be heard riding past the house, and he was even known to appear at the door. Witnesses who saw him testified that the headless horseman did not sit straight in the saddle, but rather slumped to one side; the hoofmarks of his horse, when discovered, were not the normal horseshoe shape, but plain, round indentations, as though made by stilts.

Even the sea was no barrier to the terrible horseman. A few Lochbuie Maclaines settled on the island of Tiree, where they too received a visitation from their ghostly kinsman at the hour of their deaths. On such occasions, Ewen would cross to Tiree from Port-nahaven, using the lonely Treshnish Isles as stepping-stones.

Only one individual ever cheated him of his prey. This was a very strong man, a Maclean, who met the headless horseman one night on the road between Calachyle and Salen, on the east coast of Mull. The spectre caught hold of Maclean to carry him off, but the terrified man had the presence of mind to grasp desperately at a birch sapling. Drawing on all his considerable strength, he was able to keep a grip on the tree despite Ewen's efforts to drag him away from it. During the struggle, the birch got terribly twisted and soon Maclean realised, to his despair, that its roots were being torn out, one by one. Just as the last root was giving way, a cock-crow signalled dawn, whereupon the ghost vanished. For years afterwards the twisted birch-tree was pointed out by local people.

For all others, however, there was no escape. So, the phantom horseman of Mull became the most dreaded apparition in the West Highlands. On stormy nights the islanders would listen fearfully, wondering whether the wind was playing tricks with their hearing, or the headless rider on his black horse was indeed galloping through Glen More, from Strathcoil to Pennyghael. Then, if they were of the blood of the Maclaines of Lochbuie, they would shudder at the knowledge that, before dawn, one of their number must leave this life; for Ewen of the Little Head never rode home without taking one of his kin back with him into eternity.

The Kilnure Corpse

At Fincharn, near the southern end of Loch Awe, there once lived a tailor, a very sceptical man who stubbornly refused to believe in ghosts. So his neighbours issued the traditional challenge to such folk, by daring him to go to the nearby graveyard at Kilnure, during the dead of night, and bring back the skull that lay in the window of the old church there.

The tailor, however, disdained this slight task and offered to do better than that: he would sew a pair of trews, inside the church, between dusk and cock-crow that very night. His neighbours were delighted with this suggestion and so it was agreed. At ten o'clock, therefore, the tailor took his place in the church and selected, as his makeshift work-bench, a flat gravestone resting on four low pillars. With a lighted candle at his side, he then began the monotonous task of making the trews.

For an hour, he sewed diligently, keeping his spirits up in that

gloomy place by whistling and singing the most cheerful songs he could remember.

Midnight came and went, but nothing happened to disturb his tranquillity. Not very long after twelve, however, he heard a noise coming from a gravestone near the door of the church and, looking round, he could have sworn that he saw the earth moving beneath it. A moment's reflection convinced him that this was an illusion created by the flickering of the candle, so he shrugged his shoulders and went back to his work, singing away.

Moments later, he was startled to hear a hollow voice from under the same gravestone say: 'See the great, mouldy hand, looking so hungry, tailor!' And, sure enough, a skeletal hand appeared out of the tomb. But the tailor mustered his courage and replied defiantly, 'I see that, and I will sew this.' With these words, he resumed his sewing and his singing.

A little later, the same unearthly voice called out, louder than before: 'See the great, mouldy skull, looking so hungry, tailor!'

'I see that, and I will sew this,' the tailor replied resolutely. And he plied his needle more quickly and sang more loudly.

Then the voice, sounding more ominous and reverberating around the empty church, cried out: 'See the great, mouldy shoulder, looking so hungry, tailor!'

The tailor answered calmly, 'I see that, and I will sew this.' But he sewed still more quickly and lengthened the span of his stitches.

Gradually, more and more of the corpse emerged from the grave, the dead man's haunch and, finally, his foot appearing. 'See the great, mouldy foot,' the terrifying voice snarled, 'looking so hungry, tailor!'

Although the tailor replied as before, 'I see that, and I will sew this,' he knew it was time to be gone.

He hastily completed the three last stitches, knotted the thread and broke it off with his teeth. Then he snatched up the completed trews, blew out the candle and dashed towards the door. The corpse pursued him and, as the tailor ran out across the threshold, aimed a blow at him which missed, but left the grisly imprint of its hand and fingers on the door-jamb for years afterwards. At that same moment, the cocks in Fincharn crowed for dawn and the dead man had to return to the tomb. As for the tailor, he went back to his neighbours, triumphantly bearing the trews he had made, but no longer disbelieving in the supernatural.

A Phantom Motor-Car

The ritual ingredients of ghost stories are familiar to everyone: headless horsemen, skeletons, corpses rattling chains, daggers and goblets. In short, the objects which feature in hauntings are either the artifacts of the past or timeless things which do not tie down the apparition to any particular period. At any rate, it is certainly rare for inventions of modern technology to figure in ghostly visitations.

There is a mystery in one Highland glen, however, which must be of relatively recent origin, since the apparition seen there by many witnesses is a phantom motor-car. The old road through Glen Shiel, as it wound westward to Kintail from Loch Cluanie to Loch Duich, was a hazardous drive for motorists. It was so narrow that when another car was sighted travelling in the opposite direction it was necessary to draw in at one of the passing-places or lay-bys to allow the other vehicle to pass.

Earlier this century, a number of motorists reported an identical, inexplicable experience on the old Glen Shiel road. They would see a car travelling towards them in the far distance, which almost immediately disappeared round a bend in the road — there was nothing peculiar about this, since the road was so twisting. The well-mannered driver would immediately look for a passing-place and draw into it, to await the oncoming vehicle. Mysteriously, it failed to materialise, nor did anyone ever come across it on resuming the journey.

This took place on an isolated road, with no turn-offs or farm-tracks which could have concealed the other vehicle. At night, the apparition took the form of oncoming headlights which would similarly vanish behind a bend, never to reappear. Many local people did not experience this phenomenon, but a number did — too many to be dismissed as a fanciful or superstitious minority. One visitor to the district, who saw the apparition twice, was a professor from Glasgow University and very much a man of reason. What makes the matter more baffling is that there does not seem to be any local tradition, such as a fatal accident, which would even attach a supernatural logic to the phenomenon. Now that a new road has been built, it may be that the apparition will not reappear. In any case, the phantom motor-car of Glen Shiel remains one of the more puzzling, if minor, supernatural traditions in the Highlands, already so well enriched with spectres and mysteries down the centuries.